DEADLY WARNING

Longarm rose to his full ominous height, cocked his Winchester, and shouted, "*Congelos, muchachos!*"

Some old boys just never took well-meant advice seriously. But after Longarm downed the fool who'd tried to swing his gun clear around from north to south along with the one who'd been way too fidgetsome for Longarm's taste, the two survivors were frozen stiff and pale enough to pass for snowmen on the Sonora Desert.

But then one of the rurales got stupid and started to thaw. He didn't actually swing the muzzle of his Schofield .45 Longarm's way. Longarm never gave him a chance.

* * *

Also in the LONGARM series from Jove

LONGARM
LONGARM AND THE LONE STAR LEGEND
LONGARM AND THE LONE STAR BOUNTY
LONGARM AND THE LONE STAR RUSTLERS
LONGARM AND THE LONE STAR DELIVERANCE
LONGARM IN THE TEXAS PANHANDLE
LONGARM AND THE RANCHER'S SHOWDOWN
LONGARM ON THE INLAND PASSAGE
LONGARM IN THE RUBY RANGE COUNTRY
LONGARM AND THE GREAT CATTLE KILL
LONGARM AND THE CROOKED RAILMAN
LONGARM ON THE SIWASH TRAIL
LONGARM AND THE RUNAWAY THIEVES
LONGARM AND THE ESCAPE ARTIST
LONGARM IN THE BIG BURNOUT
LONGARM AND THE TREACHEROUS TRIAL
LONGARM AND THE NEW MEXICO SHOOT-OUT
LONGARM AND THE LONE STAR FRAME
LONGARM AND THE RENEGADE SERGEANT
LONGARM IN THE SIERRA MADRES
LONGARM AND THE MEDICINE WOLF
LONGARM AND THE INDIAN RAIDERS
LONGARM AND THE HANGMAN'S LIST
LONGARM IN THE CLEARWATERS
LONGARM AND THE REDWOOD RAIDERS
LONGARM AND THE DEADLY JAILBREAK
LONGARM AND THE PAWNEE KID
LONGARM AND THE DEVIL'S STAGECOACH
LONGARM AND THE WYOMING BLOODBATH
LONGARM IN THE RED DESERT
LONGARM AND THE CROOKED MARSHAL
LONGARM AND THE TEXAS RANGERS
LONGARM AND THE VIGILANTES
LONGARM IN THE OSAGE STRIP
LONGARM AND THE LOST MINE
LONGARM AND THE LONGLEY LEGEND
LONGARM AND THE DEAD MAN'S BADGE
LONGARM AND THE KILLER'S SHADOW
LONGARM AND THE MONTANA MASSACRE
LONGARM IN THE MEXICAN BADLANDS
LONGARM AND THE BOUNTY HUNTRESS
LONGARM AND THE DENVER BUST-OUT
LONGARM AND THE SKULL CANYON GANG
LONGARM AND THE RAILROAD TO HELL
LONGARM AND THE LONE STAR CAPTIVE
LONGARM AND THE GOLD HUNTERS
LONGARM AND THE COLORADO GUNDOWN
LONGARM AND THE GRAVE ROBBERS
LONGARM AND THE ARKANSAS AMBUSH
LONGARM AND THE ARIZONA SHOWDOWN
LONGARM AND THE UTE NATION
LONGARM IN THE SIERRA ORIENTAL
LONGARM AND THE GUNSLICKS
LONGARM AND THE LADY SHERIFF

TABOR EVANS

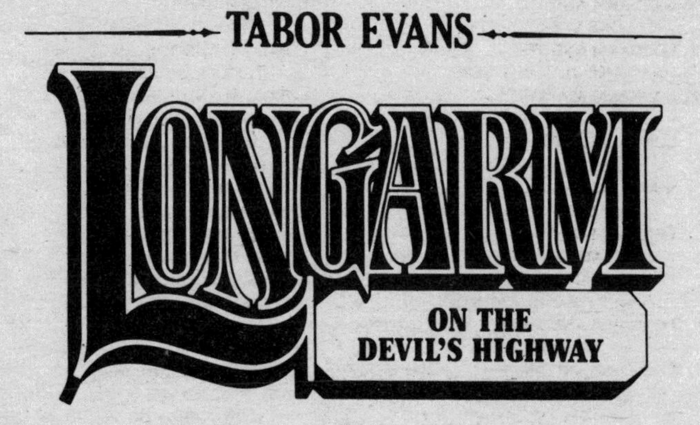

JOVE BOOKS, NEW YORK

LONGARM ON THE DEVIL'S HIGHWAY

A Jove Book / published by arrangement with
the author

PRINTING HISTORY
Jove edition / June 1992

For information address: The Berkley Publishing Group,
200 Madison Avenue, New York, New York 10016.

ISBN: 0-515-10865-0

Jove Books are published by The Berkley Publishing Group,
200 Madison Avenue, New York, New York 10016.

PRINTED IN THE UNITED STATES OF AMERICA

10 9 8 7 6 5 4 3 2 1

LONGARM
ON THE
DEVIL'S HIGHWAY

Chapter 1

Soapy Wells was an aptly named jerkwater stop where the Southern Pacific line ran perilously close to the border. By ten that morning the desert heat had soaked through the thick adobe walls of their municipal jail. So the two men alone in the cell block had good reason to regard one another with a certain amount of distaste.

The stinking but surprisingly pleasant-looking Mex behind the bars seemed too young to die, before one read his yellow sheets and marveled at him having lived this long.

The just as sweaty but not yet stinky Anglo who'd ambled back to view the prisoner was somewhat older, way taller, and wore his black-coffee Stetson pancaked in a Colorado crush. Further down he wore a hickory workshirt, tobacco-tweed pants, and vest, and one double-action Colt .44-40 carried cross-draw. He was smiling thinly under his heroic mustache and his wide-set gray eyes were friendly as a pair of gun muzzles with no particular target in mind as he told the Mex, "I'd be U.S. Deputy Custis Long, riding for the Denver District Court's Marshal William Vail, Moreno. I reckon you know why I've come for you. But look on the bright side. It'll surely take a full six or eight weeks for 'em to try you, hear out your appeal, and hang you."

Moreno softly growled, "*No me jodas*, gringo."

The taller lawman's expression didn't change as he replied in a conversational tone. "I ain't trying to fuck about with you, old son. I am spelling out some facts of life for you. They'll be paying me the same twelve cents a mile do I deliver you in Denver comfortable or otherwise. I got me a full set of cuffs and leg irons out front with my frock coat and other possibles. On the other hand, I got five in the wheel of this old .44-40 and you look sensible enough to come along civilized and maybe wear one cuff with the other gripping an arm of your Pullman seat in the wee small hours when a man gets to nodding."

He reached into a vest pocket for a couple of three-for-a-nickel cheroots as he continued, "If you give your word you'll act sensible, I'll carry you back to Denver that casual. It's only fair to warn you I shoot to kill when a prisoner takes unfair advantage of my decent side. So what's it going to be?"

The prisoner shrugged and said, *"Por que sudar?* I got no reason for to give you a reason for to shoot me, gringo. If I told you I was not wanted in your Denver would you believe me?"

The lawman chuckled fondly and replied, "Not hardly. *Pero bueno,* the turnkey out front didn't have the authority to release you to me so I sent him to fetch someone who did. Soon as they get back we'll be on our way and, meanwhile, have a smoke on me."

The prisoner managed a grudging nod of thanks as the man who'd come to fetch him for a federal hangman handed a cheroot and waterproof Mexican match through the bars. As they both lit up, the lawman observed, "They'd better get a move on if we're to catch the eastbound as jerks water here this side of noon. They say the next one don't pass through this side of sundown and I'd sure hate to spend me a whole day in this cactus patch. What do you boys do down this way for amusement, aside from whoring and robbing trains, I mean."

Moreno shrugged and replied, *"Quien sabe?* I just got here as well. They tell me they are too proud for to serve members of my *raza* at the *chincheria* run by the wife of the town law. As for the robbing of trains, I know nothing about the robbing of trains. I am only a *vaquero,* looking for work up this way. I heard they were hiring up along the Gila, so . . ."

"Spare me the *mierda* and I won't make you listen to my own sad story," the older and wordlier man cut in.

When the prisoner insisted, *"No es mierda! Es verdad!"* the lawman blew a big fat smoke ring and began, "I meant to save my virginity for the one true love I'd meet one day, but there was this wild-eyed schoolmarm I had in the third grade and whilst I prayed and pleaded, she just wouldn't stop pawing at my fair white body until, in the end, she'd had her wicked way with me."

Before he had to come up with anything sillier they were joined by a jolly fat man with dead-oyster-colored eyes and the younger turnkey who'd been sent to fetch him. The fat one introduced himself as the town law. Nobody had suspected him of selling Bibles door-to-door. As they shook, he added, "We've heard heaps about you, Longarm. Is it true you once took on a whole cavalry column down Mexico way?"

The man called Longarm, as well as Custis Long, shrugged modestly and replied, "They started it. Billy Vail never sent me down this way this time after more than one Mex outlaw. I'd like to get me and Moreno here headed back to Denver *poco tiempo,* if it's all the same with you, ah, Constable Ganes."

The lardy lawman replied, "That's something we got to study on, Longarm. It's my understanding both the Pinkertons and the Butterfield Stage Line have handsome bounties out on this young greaser. Your boss, Marshal Vail, never mentioned federal funds posted on the same. I hope that was an oversight on his part?"

Longarm blew smoke out both nostrils but kept his tone sweetly reasonable as he replied, "It wasn't. There ain't. Uncle Sam seldom rewards direct and I sure wish folk in remote corners of this proud land paid more attention to the way bounties work."

"You ain't gonna rob us of what we got coming!" Ganes cut in, not the least bit jolly.

Longarm nodded curtly and told him, "I wasn't aiming to. I hadn't finished. If you'd read the small print on that Pinkerton and Butterfield paper you're all lathered up about you'd see they've offered the reward to anyone occasioning the arrest and *conviction* of this poor soul."

"I never *done* nothing, *hombre!*" Moreno protested through the bars.

The three lawmen ignored him as Longarm continued, "No private detective agency nor stage line is allowed to carry out proper trials and executions, Constable. Do you want to put in for that bounty money, and I don't see why you shouldn't, you'd do well to have me and this poor cuss aboard the next eastbound combination. For as you'll soon discover to your own chagrin, you won't see a dime from either the pinks or that stage line before the judge up Denver way sentences this kid you picked up to start rope dancing."

"No tienes corazón! I am innocent!" wailed Moreno.

Nobody paid him any mind that time, either. Ganes ran a thoughtful thumbnail through the stubble on one of his chins as he mused, "I dunno, Longarm. To tell the truth we was hoping the federal bounty would top either Pinkerton's or Butterfield's. They don't add up to a thousand lumped together."

Longarm shrugged and replied, "Don't look at me. You should have captured Frank and Jessie if you're in this game for fun and profit. They only have five hundred posted on Henry McCarthy aka William Bonney, aka Billy the Kid. So how much were you expecting for *this* undistinguished *pistolero,* for Pete's sake?"

"More'n five hundred," Ganes grumbled, adding with a piggy gleam in one usually dead eye. "We've heard tell the Mex state of Sonora has a hundred double eagles posted on Moreno in connection with some political views he's expressed down yonder, and ain't a double eagle worth better'n twenty U. S. dollars at the current rate of exchange?"

Longarm turned to view the prisoner with renewed respect as he decided, "Any rebel worth that much *dinero* to El Presidente Diaz must be the bee's knees at revolution. What in thunder were you up to down yonder before you got in so much trouble up *here,* Moreno?"

The young Mex smiled modestly and replied, *"Quien sabe?* If you are really the gringo *simpatico* some call El Brazo Largo, the nun-raping eater of pig shit who stole La Presdidencia off the deathbed of our sainted Juarez would no doubt pay twice as much for *you,* no?"

Longarm smiled thinly and turned back to his fellow lawmen as he said, "Remind me never to deliver no prisoners in Ciudad Mejico. I'd like to head for Denver with him, now, if it's all the same with you boys."

The two Arizonans exchanged glances. Ganes said, "We'd purely love to smell the last of the stinky young greaser, Longarm. But it ain't that simple. Did I mention the outstanding warrant the Texas Rangers have out on this wayward youth?"

Longarm counted silently to three before he growled, "This has commenced to go from ridiculous to downright dumb, Ganes. A body just arriving on the scene might say you were holding some sort of *auction* on this wanted man."

To which Ganes smugly replied, "A body sure might. So far Mexico seems the highest bidder."

"Mexico can't have him," Longarm flatly replied, adding, "My warrant, signed by a federal judge, orders you to turn him over to me and then it orders me to carry him back to Denver to stand trial in said judge's federal court on crimes too numerous to jaw about if me and Moreno mean to catch that next train out."

Ganes smiled slyly at his turnkey as he unctuously replied, "I don't recall reading my own name on that writ you showed me out front, Bob."

The turnkey grinned back, saying, "That was on account you was never mentioned by name, Boss. I only work here, but didn't that Denver court address the issue to such authority as we might have us in charge, here in Soapy Wells?"

Ganes said, "By gum, I swear you're right, Bob. Just who might this federal deputy want to see about us turning this greaser over to him? Like you, I only work here."

Longarm blew smoke out both nostrils but refrained from roaring all that bullish as he told them to spare him the rest of the stale routine, adding, "I know the ending. This ain't the first time I've had to cope with an asshole with a mail-order badge holding out for reasons of local politics or common greed, and I ain't accusing anyone here of *politics*."

"What are you fixing to do, throw down on us with that fancy sixgun?" asked the greedy Ganes with more bluster than confidence.

Longarm sighed and said, "Don't tempt me. There was a rough and ready time I'd have done just that. Since President Hayes took office on that reform ticket they even make me report to work in a three-piece suit and shoe-string necktie. If you figure you can send me all around Robin Hood's Barn on fools' errands 'til someone else shows up with cash in hand you got more figuring to do. I've had all the dumb arguments with small town J. P.'s a man might need to persuade him there has to be a better way. So I reckon I'll just get on over to your Western Union and send me some wires, now."

Ganes said to go right ahead. It was his turnkey who laughed like a jackass and volunteered the nearest public telegraph office was up the line in Douglas.

A jackass might have wondered aloud how, in that case, they'd been wiring all over about bounty money since they'd picked up the wanted man aboard a suspiciously fine pony. Longarm wasn't a jackass. So he hauled out his pocket watch, morosely consulted it, and said, "Well, at least I got time to grab a bite before that fool train stops here for water."

Bob volunteered, "You'd best hurry, then. Ever' one of our few business establishments will be shutting down 'til after three for *la siesta*, it being high summer and all."

Ganes feigned an elaborate yawn and announced, "That reminds me, I was meaning to enjoy a light repast with my old lady afore the two of us slipped betwixt the sheets for a few hours. Try the stand-up beanery near the loading chutes if you like your coffee strong and your chili hot, Longarm."

Longarm had been the youngest rider in the outfit when he'd first come out from West-By-God-Virginia after the war. So he knew how it spoiled the fun when an old boy let on they were getting under his skin with their innocent-sounding barbs. He nodded soberly and said he'd best coffee-up a heap if he meant to spend the afternoon hunting snipe in the Arizona Desert.

Leaving Moreno to languish in his patent cell for now, the three lawmen headed back out front. The turnkey sat back down at their rolltop. Ganes didn't offer to help as Longarm picked up his clumsy load, but stood by like a sport until Longarm had his saddle with bridle and other possibles lashed to its many brass fittings.

As they both strode outside, the constable couldn't help but ask if it wasn't a mite unusual for a lawman arriving by rail to transport a prisoner back the same way to show up with all that cavalry gear.

Longarm shrugged the shoulder of his gun arm, his other being too busy with the heavily laden McClellan army saddle, and explained, "A man just never knows when he might have to ride. Had Moreno escaped before I got here, or been given to some *other* son of a bitch, this saddle and Winchester might have seen more use before my chore was completed. When they send me out on a chore I like to complete it."

"We heard why they call you Longarm," said the fat man, who waved expansively to their right as they walked in step, adding, "Feel free to saddle any bronc in our remuda, out back, if you'd rather not wait for that train to Douglas and the telegraph office."

Longarm almost asked, "That far, that slow, in this heat?" before he recalled how one was supposed to react when soberly told about hoop snakes, side-hill runners, big rock candy mountains, and such. He said, "I'll study on your kind offer. Never can tell about the timetables of that infernal Southern Pacific."

So they parted friendly as two buzzing sidewinders, and just in case anyone was watching Longarm really toted his load on up to the corrals and ramps alongside the railroad's water tower where, sure enough, he found a dinky tin-roofed *cafetin* that smelled way finer than it looked. The old gray-haired mestiza presiding behind the counter looked out at him less Apache once he'd ordered in Spanish.

As she glopped a heroic ladle of chili con carne over two sinister tamales made from blue cornmeal she observed few *yanquis* seemed to know how to order on such a hot day.

He explained why people not accustomed to the dry heat out their way might not grasp the advantages of breaking into a serious sweat after consuming red pepper in medicinal quantities. Her coffee was black and bitter as buffalo bile, too. Just the way he liked it when he wasn't fixing to sleep for a spell.

Once he'd calmed the rumbles in his gut and given his brains a good poke in the ass, he toted his load over to what had to be the railroad's dispatch shed. Nobody but a railroad would have built anything that substantial out of painted lumber instead of 'dobe in these parts.

The old cuss who answered Longarm's door knock sort of reminded one of a boiled lobster, albeit he'd probably been more baked than boiled so far, this morning, in that thin-walled shed. Staring in past the old coot, Longarm could see the rows of wet-cell electric batteries on a shelf above the dispatch desk. But Longarm had been raised polite, so he said, "Howdy. I'd be U. S. Deputy Custis Long and I'll bet you a silver dollar you don't wire up and down the right of way with your very own telegraph set."

The old timer said, "You lose and after that it's a dime a word, same as Western Union, if you're trying to get me to send private messages betwixt railroading transmissions."

Western Union charged a nickel a word and Billy Vail asked his field men to keep their wires short at those rates.

But there were times to argue and there were times a man just had to grit his teeth and pay up, as Miss Silver Heels used to say up in Leadville, and so Longarm set down his load and reached in his pants as he stepped on inside.

The dispatcher, who really shouldn't have, showed him to a barrel in one corner and handed him a pad and pencil, saying, "Take your time and make sure you got it just right. I got to send me a heap of earlier messages afore I can send your'n, now that things are a mite calmer along the line, what with *la siesta* coming on."

Longarm didn't ask dumb questions as the crusty but not unkind old man sat back down and proceeded to scan earlier sheets torn off the same pad Longarm was holding. Longarm idly wondered how his newfound telegraph clerk and at least a few confederates working for Western Union worked out the split. He didn't really care. He began to compose his own terse message to Billy Vail as the railroad dispatcher began to transmit a desperate request for money back East from some young lady who didn't seem to be getting married to that big *ranchero* after all.

Longarm knew this because if push came to shove he was capable of sending and receiving Morse himself. It was one of the less lethal skills he'd picked up during his short but very educational military career. He didn't really care about some dumb gal who'd traipsed all the way out here from Alabam' to wed a cuss she'd never seen. He just found it impossible not to listen while the old cuss transmitted with a clear but hesitant fist, as if he might be commencing to get stiff.

Longarm was composing his own message with the care suggested. He knew everyone in a small town knew everyone else. But he knew Billy Vail would savvy as much. So it wasn't too tough to compose a mild message about an utter son of a bitch. Billy Vail would call old Ganes that and more, once he figured just why Longarm wouldn't be heading back with Moreno on the very next train. The older but just as determined U. S. Marshal wouldn't need instructions as to how one might build a fire under a local lawman from a distance. Longarm assumed his boss would start by swearing out a federal warrant on the charge of obstructing justice. It would never stick in court after Ganes handed Moreno over with protestations of innocence, but that was the way the ploy worked, so . . .

So why was that cuss at the table sending something about Brazo Largo in Spanish, now?

Longarm listened closer. The old bastard wasn't simply telling someone he was here in this dinky border town. He was telling *los rurales,* in Agua Prieta, Sonora, less than a day's hard ride from here.

If there was one thing *los rurales* were good at, aside from the slaughter of innocents, riding had to be it. But Longarm knew he had a pretty good lead on 'em if they started before they got to the end of that treacherous wire. Meanwhile the dispatcher didn't seem to know who was listening in. So Longarm just sat there, listening, until the old timer sent a grammatical error nobody who savvied a lick of Spanish should have. It made Longarm feel kinder to the old coot, knowing he was only transmitting letter for letter without knowing the full content.

But just in case the old cuss hadn't known the Morse for O from that for A, which hardly seemed likely, Longarm changed the name he'd meant to sign from Long to Gilfoyle. Billy Vail would know he hadn't sent Deputy Gilfoyle clean to Arizona Territory. But should anyone ask this old dispatcher, it might confuse everyone in *these* parts for a spell. Longarm suspected he didn't have all that long a spell to work with, now.

Hoping Billy Vail would be able to play things by ear until such time as it might be safe to tell him what was really going on, Longarm paid the old cuss off, said something about looking for a place to sleep off the *siesta,* and headed back the way he'd come with his load.

The sun was blazing down from on high, casting mighty little shade on either side of the dusty deserted street. That was why it was deserted. Neither Anglos nor Hispanics out this way observed the custom of *la siesta* because they were lazy. It just made no sense to go out in the high summer sun of the Southwest between say noon and midafternoon unless one had to. Those newspaper jokes about frying eggs on a plank walk were no jokes in Arizona Territory. The old boys had lots of fun betting dudes who doubted a desert rattler or Gila monster could die of sunstroke, pent in the open with the sun directly overhead. Longarm was sure glad he'd eaten all that red pepper by the time he'd made it to the shade of the stable behind the jail. The sweat pouring out of him dried as if he thought he was a hot stove, which he did as he forked his McClellan over the rail of a stall and assured the proddy ponies inside of his good intent.

He was lying, of course. But how were horses supposed to know that?

It was way easier to choose two likely-looking mounts and saddle 'em up with his .44-40 holstered than it might have been the other way. He put his own saddle aboard a big blue gelding. He picked a paint for Moreno as likely the next best mount on hand. They had an even wider choice of saddles in their tack shed. Knowing Moreno probably rode *vaquero* style, Longarm chose as low-backed an Anglo roper as they had for his prisoner. He didn't want any prisoner riding any better than he had to if things got silly.

Once he had their getaway mounts saddled and bridled, Longarm led both around to the front of the jail, drew his Winchester from its saddle boot down the right side of his McClellan, and strode on in to get it over with.

He found the same young turnkey alone, half asleep, at the desk. As the kid blinked owlishly up at him, Longarm gently but firmly shoved the muzzle of his Winchester into the folds of the surprised kid's dark shirt to softly say, "I like you too much to blow your liver out your ass, Bob. So what say we start with you unbuckling that gunbelt with your left hand whilst you show me how high you can reach with the other?"

The turnkey was quick to obey, even as he protested, "Have you been smoking something stronger than Mary

Jane, Longarm? I thought we was supposed to be on the same side!"

Longarm waited until Bob's holstered S&W had thudded to the tile floor between his seat and the desk before he growled, "I thought we were as well, you treacherous mother, and I don't mean mother dear! On your feet and back to the cell block, keys and all."

Bob rose from his chair, keeping his hands polite as he gingerly picked up the key ring from the desk, observing, "Anything you say, but Constable Ganes ain't gonna like this."

Longarm said, "That's fair. I don't like him. You know what I'm doing here. Let's do it."

The turnkey gulped and led the way back. Moreno rose from his hardwood bunk with a thoughtful frown as they approached. He seemed even more puzzled as Bob opened his cell door. But he grinned with understanding and put on his big sombrero when Longarm prodded Bob inside with the one gun and held the .44-40 on him, saying, *"Vamanos pa'l carajo!"*

"You must be El Brazo Largo!" The young Mex chortled as he stepped out to let Longarm slam the cage door on the turnkey, lock it, and tell him the key ring would be on his desk.

As Longarm herded him out the front way, Moreno asked, innocently, "Are you helping me escape for *La Causa?"*

To which Longarm could only reply with a bitter laugh, "Not hardly. The *chulos chingado* were fixing to sell us *both* to *los rurales* so's we could hang together down Mexico way. But now I aim to get you up to Colorado to swing by yourself if it's all the same with you."

Chapter 2

"A 'onde vamanos?" his prisoner asked again as Longarm swung them both south from the eastbound railroad right of way they'd been following for the better part of an hour.

It hadn't been easy. Neither of their steel-shod mounts had cottoned to the uncertain feel of clinksome railroad ballast under them as Longarm had insisted on a ball-busting but mile-eating trot. But now they were well clear of Soapy Wells, and, stare back that way as he might, Longarm saw neither signs of pursuit nor hoof-mark for the lazy sons of bitches to follow, once they got around to trying.

They'd turned off where a shallow wash paved with potato-sized cobbles gave them a fair crack at working well clear of the tracks before they left signs in the desert pavement betwixt the greasewood clumps and cactus trees all about. Longarm waited 'til they were out of sight from the tracks. Then he waved at a nearby acre or more of eight-to-twelve-foot prickle pear and announced, "We'll shade and water as best we can in yonder pear 'til it cools down to endurable. Soon as the shadows lengthen a mite we'll be on our way south to Sonora, of course."

"Por que?" The young Mex protested, switching back to English lest Longarm miss his meaning, as he warned, "Is nothing down that way but El Camino Diablo, or The

Devil's Highway, as you might call it if it was on any map in either language."

Longarm didn't ask why Mexicans called something a devil's highway if it wasn't worth mapping. They called that bad stretch of desert between Las Cruces and the upper Rio Grande La Jornada del Muerto, or The Journey of Death, being such poetic folk.

Longarm had ridden part of the route—it wasn't clearly defined enough to call a trail—on an earlier case. He wasn't sure he wanted to forge eastward along that stretch. The last time he'd looked, the Yaqui had been on the warpath and while he got along with some Indians, even some Yaqui, he knew both *los federales* or Mexican Cavalry and *los rurales* or Mexico's rude answer to the Texas Rangers would be out in force in hopes of putting down the Yaqui.

Mexicans tended to be dreamers as well as romantic. The Yaqui were sort of leftover Aztec who'd never knuckled under yet and tended to scare the shit out of Apache.

Once they'd ridden well into the pear patch, Longarm dismounted first. With his Winchester held casually, he told his prisoner, "You can get down and rest your ass and pony a spell. But I'd be much obliged if you'd use that pig sticker riding betwixt your shoulder blades to cut and peel some cactus pads for our mounts whilst I tell you a couple of interesting tales."

Moreno hesitated, smiled sheepishly, and reached up to draw the eight-inch blade none of those other lawmen had thought a wayfaring stranger might have in reserve under the back of his homespun cotton *camisa*. Nobody had to tell even a part-time *vaquero* how to prepare spiny but juicy cactus pads for thirsty men or beasts. As he cut and peeled with ominous skill Longarm resisted the impulse to reach for a smoke this early and began, "I've carried many an old boy in to stand trial in the six or eight years I've been riding for the Justice Department. Hardly any of 'em ever said they were guilty, but I have to allow some gave more convincing performances than others."

"I am innocent. I know nothing of any stinking mail train they say I robbed in el estado Colorado. I have never been in your *chingado* Colorado, unless we are speaking of el rio or desierto to the northwest of here."

"I ain't finished." Longarm cut in, adding, "You may not buy this, coming from such a strict country, but U. S. federal courts have been known to find folk Not Guilty on rare occasions and, even *do* they find you guilty and sentence you to hang, you'd be surprised how often the higher court who hears your automatic appeal cuts your rope dance lesson down to Life At Hard or less. They say Judge Parker over to Fort Smith is upset as hell about that, too."

Moreno began to hand-feed juicy green mush to the big blue without being told to as he grumbled, "I do not wish for to do any time at all for a train I never saw. I know some say I did it. They must have been talking about another Juan Moreno, curdle the milk of their mothers!"

Longarm pursed his lips thoughtfully and said, "Well, there's an amazing number of John Browns who did something odd in English. Aside from the one who keeps mouldering in that grave, I read somewhere a young minuteman killed by the redcoats on Lexington Green was named John Brown and I'll allow it wouldn't have been fair to hang *him* for jayhawking in Kansas with them other Browns. So that's my very point, Moreno. If you're innocent as you claim you got nothing to fear in going back to Denver with me."

He just had to have that smoke and, dammit, there were two of them and less than a dozen cheroots to last to the next damned town or trading post. He swore under his breath, got out two with his free hand, and held one out to his prisoner, growling, "Stick this in your face and pay attention. Hoping you got what I just said about a fair trial in mind, I got another tale to tell."

He gripped his own cheroot between bared teeth and showed a Mex how to thumbnail a Mexican match aflame with one hand. As he lit both their smokes, he continued, "I made a deal a spell back with another gent, this one an

Anglo outlaw, when *los rurales* seemed out to kill us both. The deal was for the two of us to work together so's I could carry him back alive and well to face his own judge and jury. *He* kept saying he was innocent, too. I lost a heap of confidence in that old boy when he double-crossed me and got clean away."

Moreno held his own smoke with his teeth as he began to peel more cactus. Longarm took a deep drag, let it out, and quietly continued, "I reckon he figured, having a good lead on me in the land of the unfree, where *I* was wanted by the law more than *he* was, he'd escape from gringo justice, permanent."

The young Mex smiled softly and murmured, "Was that the time they still sing of, when El Brazo Largo shot it out with a whole squad of *rurales*?"

The taller lawman shook his head modestly and said, "That was in connection with another case entire. This escape artist I'd like you to keep in mind ran all the way south to Ciudad Mejico and I don't mind saying I had me a time catching up with the sneaky son of a bitch without I got my own ass shot off. But I did. Are you with me so far?"

Moreno grimaced and said, *"Sí,* you brought the *sinverguenza* back and then they hung him, no?"

"No," said Longarm, soberly. "I rid back to Denver *alone* in the end. But, like I said, justice had been done, if you follow my drift."

Moreno chuckled dryly and replied, "You have my word I shall not try for to escape without giving the matter much thought. Are we to wait until dark and see if we can make the safer surroundings and more reasonable transportation at this time of the year? I do not think these *caballos* could carry us much farther than perhaps the less crooked lawmen at Tombstone."

Longarm said, "Take care of your own mount whilst you're about it. I was hoping even a stranger in these parts would figure a hard night's ride across the desert to Tombstone made the most sense."

"But does it not?" Moreno insisted.

Longarm nodded but explained, "Them two-faced sons of bitches out to do us both dirt can beat us most anywhere sensible by Morse Code. I know for a fact they've alerted *rurales* at Aqua Prieta and that's why we're holed up in this pear instead of riding on East. I don't know who Constable Ganes takes his orders from. But it has to be somebody higher up the county totem pole, and we got us over forty miles of Cochise County betwixt us and anywhere else, minimum, on the Americano side of the border. They might or might not have confederates as far east as El Paso or as far west as Nogales. They can surely beat us to either railroad bottleneck by train and I like to hold my escaping to a minimum."

He took another deep drag, glanced up at the glaring desert sun, and said, "I figure our best bet would be a discreet cross-country run for the Sea of Cortez. We can catch either a boat or train out of there, depending on who's watching what."

Moreno almost dropped the cheroot from his slack jaw as he stared at Longarm thundergasted. Longarm nodded and said, "I know it sounds *lerdo*. That's why it might not be. Nobody will be expecting anyone smart as me to haul a prisoner wanted in Denver that far, the wrong way entire, see?"

"I thought you just said you were familiar with El Camino Diablo," the Mexican soberly replied.

Longarm nodded but allowed, "Maybe not as far west as that. I covered the Sonora Desert I know best in connection with outlaws sticking closer to the Sierra Madre to the southeast."

Moreno said, "*Mierda,* you do not know El Camino Diablo at all. Is more the difference between being only a little lost or lost forever than a trail. Even the Yaqui have to pick their way carefully and if you have only been among the foothill canyons of the Sierra Madre you have not really been on El Camino Diablo and listen to me, El Brazo Largo, this is late *agosto,* the most *peligroso* time of the year for to cross any *desierto,* and El Camino Diablo is no *desierto*. El Camino Diablo is what you might get if you stuffed a bake oven with broken glass and venomous creatures before you poured tar and vinegar all over it. I am speaking of El Camino Diablo in the *wet* season, of course. Nobody could get across alive in this dry season."

Longarm nodded and said, "*Esta bien*. Like I just said, nobody will be expecting us to ride that way."

The Mex made the sign of the cross with the tip of his knife and insisted, "*Ay, sin falta*. Listen, forget what I said about heat, thirst, scorpions, and reptiles. Did I fail to mention the lava flats that stretch endlessly like lumpy mattresses of broken glass, where the ground lies reasonably flat? Most of El Camino Diablo crosses what you might call rolling country, if you considered a gentle rise ending in an unexpected cliff a *roll*. Where the country has not been covered by lava or eroded down to bedrock by mindless flash floods, it lies under sand dunes. *Muy grande* sand dunes that sing like ghosts as they shift with the night winds and change shape in order to confuse a traveler by the light of dawn. Is impossible for to cross without getting lost at least a little. This can be bad enough when there is water to be found here and there. At this time of the year water is most impossible for to find, even when you know where you are."

"I wish you'd water them ponies with cactus juice instead of crying about dying of thirst," Longarm cut in, shifting the Winchester thoughtfully as he added, "I know this may surprise an old desert rat like you, but some renegade Mormons tried to strand me in the middle of The Great Salt Desert one time and, as you can plainly see, I'm still here."

Moreno tried. "*Salud*. I spit on your gringo *desiertos*. It might be possible for to follow El Camino Diablo at this time of the year if we had the right *mierda*. *Pero* we do not. We got one canteen for to go with each saddle. You got your bedroll and what else on that army saddle that came with you. I lack so much as a poncho and it gets *cold* on El Camino Diablo after dark."

Longarm said, "I got a blanket I can spare you in my bedroll but you got a point about grub and water. I got the day or more's supply of canned beans and tomato preserves I like to keep on hand. I even got enough soap for us both in a saddlebag. Toting along enough water is the problem. I'd feel better if we had us more grub and at least one spare pony to fall back on. Can't always count on cactus juice in really bad country, and there's just no way to tell how much a mount might have in him before you push him all the way. I had a pony founder under me up Death Valley way one time. I don't mind telling you I was mighty footsore before I got out of *that* particular fix. You say we got to cross *lava* as well as loose sand in serious quantities?"

Moreno cut another cactus pad as he morosely replied, "If we ride for the West Coast. If we try to circle south of *los rurales* to the east we only got to ride over Yaqui, *muy* upset about something else El Presidente must have done to them. Yaqui, as you must know, are *muy malo,* even when they are not upset. *Pero* their country is not as hard on hooves as the country further west. Perhaps that is for why it is their country. The only *Indios* who manage to get by during the rainy season between here and the Sea of Cortez would be what your *raza* calls diggers. Is more polite for to call them Pima, or Yuma, if that is what they wish."

Longarm said, "I call 'em Pima, or mayhaps Ho, just meaning folk, if I ain't too clear about their nation. I got no disrespect for folk who can keep themselves and even their kids alive in country many a grasshopper might starve in. Most Pima are right decent. Papago, too."

Moreno shrugged and said, *"Sí, pero* one feels less comfortable around Yuma, and some Yuma do roam south for to gather salt and shells."

Then the young Mex laughed and asked, "For why am I worried about us getting killed by Yuma for our boots? Is no way we can get so far without more *mierda,* a lot more *mierda,* no?"

Longarm decided, "When you're right you're right. But *los rurales* pack plenty of shit along in the field. I doubt that bunch our old pal Ganes wired will be coming to pick us up by train. They ain't supposed to hunt on *our* side of the border any more than I'm allowed to hunt *south* of the border, right?"

Moreno nodded dubiously but said, "They do, and so do you, El Brazo Largo. Is that not for why they posted that *dinero* on your gringo head?"

Longarm smiled thinly and replied, "That's the point I was about to make, if only you'd just hesh. On those rare occasions I just have to invade Mexico I try to do so *discreet*. Assuming them *rurales* on their way to Soapy Wells are half as discreet as me, they'll want to ride west, south of the border, to just south of Sour Wells, where their pal Ganes won't make a fuss about 'em crossing."

Moreno looked around nervously and dropped his voice almost to a whisper as he said, "*Ay, caramba, we* are just north or just south of the border, even as we stuff these *caballos* with *cacto*, no?"

Longarm was grinning wolfishly as he replied, "Yep. Shut up and tend the ponies whilst I study on ambushing the dirty bastards."

Chapter 3

Uncle Sam had won everything north of the Gila fair and square in the Mexican War and that would have been the end of it if the railroad surveyors had been able to find a route to California down the north banks of the westward trending river. But they hadn't. So a railroad promoter named Jim Gadsden had talked President Pierce into calling him some sort of diplomat. Then along about 1853 he'd talked Mexico into selling him around forty-odd thousand extra square miles of its northern desert range for ten million dollars of the U. S. taxpayer's money.

The U.S. taxpayer had been so pissed off that President Pierce had had to fire old Jim Gadsden. But by then the deed had been done. So now the border ran string straight, unfenced and unmarked, just south of the more curvaceous railroad and, as Longarm had recalled from earlier troubles in those parts, a narrow Mex trail wound through the chaparral out of sight of the official border. For cow thieves, smugglers, or worse just never knew where they might want to cross into Arizona Territory from the state of Sonora.

Longarm had guessed right about the *rurales* coming to get him and his own prisoner, too. They'd have never been on that trail at this hour in the afternoon had not they left their border post to the east before anyone had been able to wire their *capitano* about more recent developments. But since they had, they were loping along, as off guard as *rurales* ever got, feeling secure in their misguided belief they'd have a gringo Judas or more to aid and abet their capture of El Brazo Largo once they got to Soapy Wells around sundown.

But even at their most relaxed they were strung out and bouncing all about in their tall gray hats and crossed bandoliers. So as they were passing yet more pear Longarm had chosen south of their trail, a shot rang out to empty all four saddles *poco tiempo*.

Nobody had been hit, yet. *Rurales* were just too well trained in gunslickery to leave any sky outlining them once someone else had chosen them as targets. They'd practiced this basic field maneuver before. Longarm had hoped they might have.

That was how come he was hunkered in some greasewood just *north* of the trail when Moreno fired his derringer behind some cholla south of it. As both Longarm and his prisoner had hoped they might, *los rurales* hit the dirt in running crouches, the last in line gathering the grounded reins of all four ponies to lead them clear as the other three fanned out along the trail, screened from their south, guns drawn, while they awaited Moreno's next move.

Moreno couldn't move worth mention, handcuffed to a stout greasewood stem where Longarm had left him with that double derringer he kept for unexpected events such as this one.

So Longarm was the one who rose to his own ominous height behind them, cocked Winchester at port, to shout, *"Congelos, muchachos!"* in a distinctly serious tone.

Some old boys just never took well-meant advice seriously. But after Longarm had downed the asshole who'd tried to swing his own gun clean around from south to north in time, along with the one who'd been way too fidgetsome to Longarm's taste, the one holding the ponies and the survivor on the trail were frozen stiff and almost pale enough to pass for snowmen on the Sonora Desert.

Longarm said, in Spanish, "Pay attention and you may live to fuck your mothers some more after all. First I would like to see you on the trail to show me how far you can throw that pistol in your hand."

The *rurale* didn't actually swing the muzzle of his Schofield .45 Longarm's way. Longarm never gave him the chance. When he saw the hesitation in the other man's eyes, he fired from the hip to send the Mex backwards into some cat-claw with two rounds of .44-40 in his upper chest. The *rurale*'s sixgun and big hat fell to the dust. The *rurale* didn't. Cat-claw was like that when it got a good grip on something with its countless thorns.

The last *rurale* was sobbing like a frightened kid and pissing down one leg of his gray whipcord pants as he raised his free hand and a fistful of pony reins skyward, pleading, "Do not kill me, El Brazo Largo!"

So Longarm said, "I was hoping you might have guessed who I am. It saves us both some boasting. Unbuckle your gunbelt with your left hand. Make sure you hold on to those *caballos*."

The *rurale,* the obvious baby of the outfit, did exactly as he was told. Longarm had already noticed the four *rurale* mounts were trained not to spook at the sound of gunfire. It took a steady mount to shoot up the peasantry *rurale* style.

Once he'd disarmed the pants pisser, Longarm had him tether the ponies to some greasewood. Then he frog-marched him north to where he'd left the two ponies from Soapy Wells. He pointed the still warm muzzle of the Winchester at the paint, still wearing the roping saddle he'd helped himself to for his prisoner. He told this one, "Untie that pinto, mount it, and ride. If you look back, or if I ever see you again, for that matter, your poor old mother will just have to play with herself with a corn cob if she can't get the *pigs* to fuck her. *You* won't ever see her again."

"There is no need for to rub it in," the *rurale* sighed weakly, weak with relief at the thought he might live after all. As he untethered the paint with shaky hands he murmured, "I take it El Brazo Largo has a message for my superiors?"

Longarm chuckled and replied, "Let them get their own mothers. I'm not letting you go to prove a point. If those others knew who I was they should have known I don't shoot anyone who does exactly what I tell him to do. They didn't. You did. So now you get to ride on back to your post. For by the time you can get there my prisoner and me will be halfway to the Gila. So what are you waiting for, a farewell kiss?"

The young *rurale* forked himself gracefully aboard the strange saddle and scrub pony to light out at full gallop, not looking back but unable to resist one of those *loco* rooster laughs, once he was well out of rifle range.

Longarm didn't care. He'd given the asshole the message he wanted all those other assholes to hear, hoping they'd buy it as a slip.

Having gotten that business out of the way, Longarm reloaded his Winchester from the reserve ammo in one saddlebag. Then he untethered the big blue and led it south through the stickerbrush. When it spooked at the smell of blood near the trail, Longarm soothed, "Don't get your bowels in an uproar, you nutless and brainless waste of good oats. Dead *rurales* can't shoot women and livestock to win medals, and you might be on your way home to your own stable tonight if you don't make me shoot you."

His tone of voice, if not his intent, soothed the gelding enough to handle as he led it to the four *rurale* mounts and tethered it with them. Then he shoved the Winchester back in its saddle boot and strode on to where he'd left Moreno and his derringer on the south side of the trail.

To nobody's surprise the young Mex was still handcuffed behind the same cover, casually holding the bitty derringer in the other hand. As Longarm approached he asked his prisoner, "How come you only fired once? I told you there were two rounds in that belly gun."

Moreno managed to look a tad more innocent than that last *rurale* Longarm had shot as he replied, "I was saving this last round in case one of those *tiros* got through you.

Are you going to leave me chained to this *arbusto chingado* all night?"

"I'd best have that loaded pissoliver back before I get within gutshot range with the handcuff key, no offense."

Moreno laughed roguishly and demanded, "*Mierda*, do you really think I would shoot an *hombre* with his own gun?"

Longarm shrugged and said, "It's been known to happen." Then he took off his hat and held it out, upside down, in both of his hands, saying, "Here, I'll make it easy for you."

Moreno hesitated, then he laughed again and asked, "Easy for to do what? For to toss this in that hat or for to shoot you with it?"

Longarm told him to just go ahead and do whatever he had a mind to. Moreno sighed and tossed the derringer Longarm's way, observing, "You knew I'd be too smart to die of thirst chained to this *arbusto,* no matter how much fun it might be, watching the *buitres y* coyotes eat your *culo,* eh?"

Longarm put his hat back on his head and refastened the derringer to one end of his watch chain as he said, "Something like that." Then he reloaded the derringer's two chambers with fresh rounds, real ones, before slipping the results in a vest pocket.

The details had not been lost on the quick-witted Moreno, who softly observed, "Hey, that was *muy liso.* You pulled the lead from both rounds and then what, some paper wadding?"

"Cheroot ends," Longarm replied laconically as he moved in with his handcuff key to unshackle his prisoner, explaining, "Firmly packed tobacco has to be good for something once you've smoked it down too short to puff on. One shot was all it took to stop them *rurales* and allow me to get the drop on 'em. So I forgive you for not firing twice, like I told you."

He helped Moreno up and refastened the cuffs to the back of his gunbelt as he said, "We'd best get cracking with our spoils of war, now. Come on. You'll see I got you a better saddle with a swell bedroll and extra canteens, once I make sure there's no concealed weapons aboard your new mount."

Moreno tried, *"Ay, Dios,* don't you ever let down your guard? I thought we just proved you could trust me with a gun, no?"

Longarm snorted in disbelief and said, *"Manjate, cabrón,* you had plenty of time to see for yourself I'd left you armed with blanks. Even if you were too dumb to look, you were right about what a dumb move it would have been."

"Mierda, I thought you were starting to like me," sighed the prisoner.

Longarm said, "I ain't getting paid to like you or not like you. It's up to the judge and jury to say what kind of a cuss you might be. So let's be on our damn way to Denver by way of El Camino Diablo, now, you sweet young thing."

Chapter 4

Longarm handcuffed his prisoner safely out of the way again as he sorted things out where he'd left the five ponies. The Springfield carbines all but that one had left aboard his mount were chambered for the U.S. issue .45-70 they fired from their Schofield cavalry pistols. Longarm threw them far and wide but just dumped the useless spare ammo in the dust and pony shit, knowing Moreno couldn't back-shoot him without anything to stick it in.

All four *rurale* mounts were chestnut geldings with at least some Barbary blood in 'em. Some held a Spanish Barb and a Spanish Arab were the same critter. Longarm had been told and had no call to doubt the Barb's spine was shorter by one vertebra, accounting for both its ball-busting trot and its ability to do so packing heavy loads. He decided he liked the lines of the one with a diamond-shaped blaze and a wire-scarred shoulder. So he unsaddled it, tossed the Mex saddle aside for now, and forked his own McClellan aboard, informing the Barb, "I admire a pony with enough sense to hit a fence sort of sideways instead of head-on. You're likely more used to that spade bit I see they shoved in your poor mouth. So I'll shove my own bridle in amid my own possibles for now."

Suiting actions to his words, he removed his bridle from the big blue he'd already unsaddled. The dumb brute just stood there, free as a bird, 'til Longarm slapped it with his Stetson, snorting, "Go home, you fool plug."

As it snorted back and loped off to the west through the chaparral, Longarm started to explain to the nearby Mex. But he never. He knew an old owlhoot rider like Moreno would have already seen the advantages of letting a less valuable mount lay a false trail across the desert pavement.

Like most of the dry country of the Southwest, where it wasn't covered with something more interesting, the bare ground tended to be encrusted most everywhere with the same desert pavement or what Hispanics called *caliche*. By either name it looked as if someone had spread roofing paper coated with birdcage gravel betwixt all the clumps of dead to gray-green vegetation. The dry winds carried away the fines and left the bigger grains of grit. The rare rains and sometimes heavy desert dew drew chalky salts to the surface to plaster all the bitty lumps together. The resulting crust was little thicker than a big old sheet of pasteboard, and so anyone or anything walking or running across desert pavement tended to leave deep prints that could be read by anyone interested for months or even years, depending on the local climate.

That blue sure left a beeline for Sour Wells from this patch most anyone could read plain enough as the end of the trail for those fool *rurales*. The one he'd spared would doubtless be back with others by the time the three cadavers they'd find hereabouts had been et entire by the buzzards and such. So they could just lay where he'd dropped 'em for all he cared.

He started to unsaddle another bay. He considered and decided the two they'd be leading as pack brutes could pack just as well or better with their riding saddles than with pack saddles he didn't have for either and it might make swapping mounts easier in a pinch.

He gathered the four filled canteens and saddlebags from the one saddle he was leaving behind. He put them aboard a pony they'd only be leading, for now. Then he went through all the saddlebags and got rid of personal crap, save for some money and a dirty book he might have time to read later. He naturally hung on to all their field rations, shelter halves, and such. He put the best bedroll in the bunch aboard the saddle of the mount he'd chosen for his prisoner. He'd noticed it fought the bit a mite and rolled its eyes like a critter that spooked easier than the other three. Other than being a mite hard to handle, it seemed strong and fast enough to pack a Mex who could turn out hard to handle in his own right.

Once he had all that out of the way he ambled over to uncuff his prisoner again, saying, "In case you ain't been watching, I picked you their best roll and worst mount. We've still got an hour or more of fair light to work with. So we're going to mosey on up to that railroad again, leaving as much sign as it might take. I bragged to their sole survivor on where we'd be beelining. So let's make it look that way as far as the tracks where we *won't* leave sign on the jagged-ass ballast and sun-silvered cross-ties."

Moreno rubbed his freed wrist as he smiled shyly and said, "I have had some experience in such *matteres*, just trying for to track stray *vacas*, of course. We ride back the way we just came for a little. Then we drop off to the south and not the north again, no?"

Longarm shook his head and said, "No. They'll likely commence their hunt for us here, mayhaps with some help from Cochise County. So they'll be scouting sharp for sign to the west. With luck they may read the tracks of that pony I turned loose the wrong way. But it's still to be a pure bitch to pussyfoot off the tracks to the west without leaving any sign at all. Mount up. I'll explain what Abe Lincoln had to say about fooling all of the people some of the time as we move out."

Moreno didn't argue, or even ask what in blue blazes Longarm had in mind until they were back up between the steel rails in the soft gloaming light. But when Longarm pointed east, toward the first star of the evening and that *rurale* outpost just over the horizon, Moreno gasped, *"No hagas fregas!* That way leads us straight to *carajo*! If we do not ride into *rurales* we could end up dancing with Yaqui in the dark!"

Longarm heeled his mount eastward, leading a second on the *reata* he'd improvised from a dead *rurale*'s tent rope, as he soothed, "We're not riding all that far. You got a point about Yaqui war parties in these parts. I've got a certain pear flat in mind as runs from nigh the tracks up a shallow draw coming down off the higher range to the south. I got away from Yaqui and worse, some mighty ornery outlaws, by way of all that cactus a spell back. It was in connection with a crooked transfer of stolen stock by way of what we called the Laredo Loop. I'd tell you more about it if I was in the business of educating yet-to-be-convicted felons. Suffice it for now to say them *rurales* coming this way with a bone to pick with us ought to lope right through that stretch of pear without scouting for a thing. They'll be fanning out to figure where we went after they get to where we ambushed that first bunch back yonder, see?"

"*Nos vamos a morir todos,* if we are lucky," Moreno sighed, making the sign of the cross as he and his own two ponies followed Longarm eastward. As his mount misplaced a steel-shod hoof on loose ballast and barely recovered without falling, the prisoner added, "Forget what I just said about them just killing us outright instead of having fun with us, you *pendejo loco!* You are going to kill us before *los rurales* or Yaqui get the chance! Is getting too dark for to ride so fast on loose *cascajo, cabrón!*"

Longarm growled, "*Estas lleno de mierda*. Horses can see better in the dark than we can and I can still see where I'm going. You sure have a heap to learn for a famous owlhoot rider, Moreno!"

His prisoner protested, "I told you I was not the Juan Moreno who robbed that *chingada* mail train. I am only a poor *vaquero,* out of work and a long way from home."

Longarm shrugged and said, "Cowhands are supposed to know which end of a horse the shit falls out of as well. Whatever you may do for a living when nobody's looking, take my word I've rid over worse footing than this, faster, by pure-ass starlight."

"You could not have been sober at the time," Moreno protested.

Longarm smiled ruefully and replied, "I'd have surely felt better at the time with a few stiff drinks in me. I was being chased through canyon country, after dark, by Mescalero."

The Mexican sniffed and retorted, "I spit on your Apaches *del Norte,* next to our own much crueler Yaqui."

Longarm shrugged and said, "Hell, there ain't no nation anyone with a lick of sense would want to be taken alive by, once they'd put on their paint and done some dancing. The point I was trying to make is that them Mescalero never caught me. That was on account I trusted my own pony in the dark more than they trusted their own."

Moreno insisted, "Don't you mean no Indio would risk riding off a cliff in the dark unless he really had to?"

To which Longarm soberly replied, "Maybe. I *had* to. Now hush and let's do some riding."

Moreno did and they did. Neither the railroad right of way nor the dirt tracks punching through north and south of the border paid any mind to the few square miles of thick but fairly friendly cactus looming all about in the starlight. A lot had likely grown back after the work gangs had cleared their original swathes and no doubt stuffed themselves and their stock with prickle pear, or *nopal*, as the juicy stuff was called in Spanish. It tasted sort of like celery might if you washed it with soap and didn't rinse it off too good.

The sort of soil it picked to grow so thick on was more important at the moment. Longarm twisted in the saddle to instruct Moreno on the fine art of drifting four ponies off railroad ballast in an easy-grazing way, as if some range strays had sort of wandered on a good old patch of shade. There was no way to avoid leaving sign near the tracks. The idea was to avoid leaving any interesting enough to *follow* for at least a few days.

Unlike greasewood and cholla, *nopal* preferred not to punch its way up through caliche. You'd find no prickle pear at all for miles and then you'd hit upon a veritable jungle of the stuff where the ground lay flatter, a tad lower, and above all free of the usual alkali salts. *Nopal* could take *some* alkali around its roots, as anyone who chewed much of the stuff could taste. But unlike salt bush, greasewood, and such, your average cactus spread its roots far and shallow for the dew water in halfway damp sweet soil. So it came as no surprise to Longarm, once they were in among the high thorny pads, to see they were on soft, dusty sand that figured to be reworked sudden by ground breezes and smaller desert critters. Once they were deep enough in the pear flat to feel more conversationsome Longarm told his prisoner, "Last time I come through here I was riding a purloined longhorn. So the Yaqui trying to trail me dismissed me for a stray cow. Don't see even their pony tracks, now, though. Of course, it was a spell back."

The Mex snorted, "Even if you could see like an owl there must be a thousand ways one could drift through all this *nopal*. So how could one hope to backtrack anything or anyone important, eh?"

Longarm chuckled and replied, "That's what I just said. We can still circle and double back a time or more as we drift these mustangs deeper into Old Mexico. As we do so I'll study on whether we ought to hole up for tomorrow near the south end of the pear flat or put some more distance between us and the border before daybreak."

Moreno didn't argue as Longarm led them in a lopsided circle around some thicker cactus and then moved on at an angle, but as a former resident of Sonora he felt obliged to point out, "Yaqui are the best night fighters on this continent. Is more usual to stay in one place after dark and ride *muy pronto* by day in Yaqui country, no?"

Longarm shrugged and said, "Just the opposite of the way you get through Apache country, or so they say. I've been jumped by Yaqui after dark and in broad day and I don't get down this way all that often. So, like I said, I'm studying."

Moreno observed, "If Yaqui see you, they are sure for to chase you. The advantage of meeting the *vero cabrónes* by daylight is that you can see them coming at you. The spawn of *El Diablo* and depraved coyotes see better in the dark than cats!"

Longarm nodded and said, "So I've been told. Speaking of old boys who can see in the dark, have you ever revolted under my old rebel pal, El Gato?"

Moreno cautiously replied, "I have heard of El Gato. They say he once cut the *cojones* off a *rurale capitano* in his own bed. The unfortunate officer woke up as El Gato was putting it to his *mujer*."

Longarm chuckled and said, "That's the way El Gato tells it, all right. I ain't sure I buy the part about the captain's wife enjoying it 'til her fool husband woke up. I wish you could have said you'd rid with El Gato's band, more personal. I'm still working on how close I got to guard you, too."

"El Gato has never raided as far north as your Colorado," the prisoner declared.

Longarm sighed and said, "I know. That's my point. I mean to take you back to Denver either way. But I'd feel more relaxed about you if I figured you figured to beat the rap. Like you said, there must be a heap of John Browns or Juan Morenos, as your folk put it more poetic. On the other hand, I'd have to be a total asshole to trust a prisoner who knew for a fact he was fixing to hang unless he got the drop on me."

Moreno chuckled and pointed out, "You got worse things for to worry about than me, El Brazo Largo. Is true a *bandido feroz* such as I might slit your throat or stab you in the back. *Pero* no *Yaqui* would be half so nice to *either* of us, eh?"

Longarm told him to shut up, adding, "We're far enough south to trot some more. So let's eat us up some distance, you cheersome cuss."

They did. It wasn't easy. Longarm in the lead could trust his mount to avoid the branching cactus in the tricky light. Since he was only human, Longarm tried to protect his own face by holding his Winchester butt-plate up out ahead of him.

It worked to some extent. Prickle pear barely prickled next to ferocious stuff like cat-claw and cholla. His bare right knuckles caught some thorns now and again, out front like that. His face suffered more from spattered seeds and over-ripe red pulp from the pears, or tunas, as the fruit of the prickle pear or *nopal* was called, depending on by whom.

Like most cactus, prickle pear flowered right after the winter rains and set fruit ripe for plucking by midsummer. By this late a lot of tunas had been plucked, pecked, or just fallen. Those still clinging to the ends of green cactus pads were more rotten than ripe by now. So smashing into 'em with a rifle butt gave much the same results as bunting rotten figs and cherries with a baseball bat. Longarm was glad he'd wrapped his frock coat with his bedding under that canvas tarp behind him. He feared the crimson stains would never come out of his shirt. Dry cleaning might in time make his dark brown pants and vest presentable by lamplight, at least.

It felt as if he'd picked himself at least a wagonload of tunas before his pony clinked a steel-shod hoof on something more serious than sand and broke stride to move slower, up a modest slope, through way lower chaparral. Longarm was just as glad to be out of all that prickle pear. But he didn't feel as good about the dotted line of distant nightfires against the ink black hills to the southeast. He could tell the otherwise featureless ridge was there because a late-rising moon was turning the sky behind it a starless shade of schoolroom slate. Longarm reined in and called back, "Hey, Moreno?"

There was no answer. A fuzzy gray critter got to its feet in Longarm's middle but turned around and lay back down when the fool Mex got around to calling back, "*Aquí,* I thought I had lost you amid all that *nopal chingado!*"

Longarm called back, "That makes two of us. Keep your voice down but get up here and tell me what you make of my greater worry."

When the native of that part of Mexico joined him, they both agreed someone over yonder had camped in numbers too numerous to be worried about giving their position away.

Moreno volunteered, "*Federales. Los rurales* never patrol in such numbers. Is probably cavalry with some field artillery for to civilize my distant Yaqui cousins, no?"

Longarm wiped at his sticky face with a pocket kerchief he'd wet with canteen water as he decided, "I doubt Yaqui or even Lakota would be camped so bold in such numbers, this late in the game. Assuming more than one officer on non com in the bunch has ever rid out after Indians before, I'd buy such a display as *bait*. You're likely right about 'em having at least a few field guns. Last I heard our own Seventh Cav has started hauling along some small bore but rifled and breech-loading Hotchkissers. Say they've strung some wire, loose and low on tent stakes just this side of all them decoy fires, and then say they got the wired and lit-up ground zeroed in with Lord-knows-what from the darkness beyond . . ."

"Were we planning to *attack* the *cabrónes* in any case?" asked his prisoner in a worried tone, having learned not to take anything for granted around this big gringo.

Longarm chuckled wistfully and replied, "I ain't even supposed to come this far south after rascals like you, more's the pity. The question before the house ain't exactly how we work our way beyond all them armed and dangerous troops. We got to make sure we don't blunder into anyone *else* admiring all that temptation from a safe distance."

Moreno gasped and declared, "*Ay, Dios mío!* What a *chingado* time for to stumble over Yaqui in the dark!"

To which Longarm could only reply, morosely, "I wish you could tell me a *good* time to meet up with Yaqui on the prod!"

Chapter 5

They made it. That hadn't been easy, either, and Longarm had nearly gunned at least two owls, countless lizards, and at least one man-sized bisnaga cactus crouching amid the greasewood ahead that froze but refused to put up its hands when Longarm threw down on it. But daybreak found them well to the south-southwest of that army camp, if that had been an army camp, in a modest canyon or big arroyo cut through the higher confusion down that way.

As it got light enough to make out colors Moreno agreed the desert fan palms grown to modest size up and down the canyon would help a heap at high noon. When he pointed out there was no water, reaching as he did so for a canteen, Longarm said, "Nobody but a total greenhorn would camp near late-summer water in hostile Indian country. But them palms say there's *some* here for them as ain't afraid of honest toil. So go ahead with that canteen and then I'll share some grub with you. Then I have some digging chores mapped out for you before it gets too warm down here betwixt these chalky walls."

Moreno protested they had plenty of water in all the canteens they'd picked up along their merry way. Longarm said there was never plenty of water on the desert in late summer. Then he started to water their ponies, using nose bags the *rurales* had brought along, thus sparing their hats.

There was plenty of the cracked corn Mex ponies were used to amid the *rurale* supplies. But Longarm saved that for a less friendly layover. He found a long pole of dead and dry saguaro-rib to knock some palm fruit down for the stock instead.

The insipid black fruit looked sort of like ripe olives but grew in bunches like grapes. So it came down in considerable amounts once Longarm was able to get at it with his literally ten-foot pole. After that it wasn't much. Indians admired the semisweet pulp of desert palm fruit and took the trouble to grind the pits into a meal some said might pass for sandy coconut meat. Horses just about went wild for anything that close to food fit for human consumption, being more used to less tasty fodder. Longarm chewed a couple of palm fruits as he chored the four ponies. They tasted just as bland as he'd remembered. As he broke out canned beans and tomato preserves for himself and his prisoner he said, "We don't have to cook this trail grub. That's why I brung it. We might risk making coffee before we leave here."

"Sí, as soon as that sun sets, no?" his prisoner tried to agree.

Longarm shook his head and said, "No. We ain't half as far from them Yaqui-haunted hills to our east as I'd like to be and the owl birds we met last night scared me enough."

He finished opening Moreno's second can with the right blade of his pocketknife and handed it over as he continued, "We're likely safe for a while here, as long as we don't make a habit of it. I already told you how come I picked this shade with no handy water. I feel even more encouraged by all that fan palm fruit I just picked for our ponies. These tuna stains on our duds are sort of encouraging as well."

Moreno asked why. Longarm scowled at him to growl, "I swear you have a lot to learn for a rider of the owlhoot trail who has to have more Indian blood in him than me! Ain't you ever noticed how *picked-over* the desert gets when there's Indians or even your own kind in walking or even jackass distance?"

Moreno brightened and dug into his beans with that pig sticker Longarm had let him hang onto, for now, as he decided, *"Es verdad.* Pima, even Yaqui, drop almost everything for to gather the rare fruits of *el desierto* in season. Since none has been gathered around here, is safe for to assume there are no Indios, eh?"

Longarm washed down some beans with tomato preserves before he pointed out, "It's never safe to assume there ain't no Indians about, as George Armstrong Custer would be the first to tell you, if he still could. But ungathered grub is a surer sign than no sign at all. It's easier for your average Indian to cover his or her tracks than it is to pass up anything sweet or salty. They don't get half as much of either flavor as they'd like and, hell, even some of *my* kind find pear fruit, or tunas, tasty."

Moreno sighed wistfully, tried some of the tomato preserves, and said, *"Ay,* Jesus, Maria *y* Jose, *la tuna* is better for to eat than this *mierda.* As plucked from the *nopal* is maybe too full of watery juice and *chingado* seeds for to make a meal for a real *hombre. Pero* have you ever enjoyed *queso de tuna,* as my people make it?"

Longarm set his empty cans aside and rose to head for the saddles drying over a nearby fallen palm log as he replied, "Sure I have, if you mean that cactus cheese you see in so many Mex markets. It's almost as tough to avoid as cactus candy and I'll allow there's way more to it. Looks like them red round cheeses the Dutch folk make, only it tastes more like petrified prune pulp."

Then he broke out a folding camper's spade, adjusted it for digging, and added, "I'll start, but don't push your luck with me. Finish your damned breakfast and get down to the water table, here, whilst I do the hard work."

Moreno polished off the last of the tomato preserves and put his knife away again. As he joined Longarm between where they'd been eating and where the big lawman had chosen to sink a well, Moreno growled, *"No tengo razón, lo se, pero* how do you intend for to work harder after I take that *chingado* shovel from you?"

Longarm handed him the tool, saying, "It's getting to be late-morning hole-up time. Anyone else in these parts who's still moving will be seeking a shady spot to cut out the same for a spell and *I* found this hidey hole by spying palm tops at sunrise, so . . ."

He blinked himself wider awake and muttered, "Damn, I never talk pointless like this when I've had my morning coffee."

Then he ambled over to the saddles again to break out his saddle gun, a canteen, and some extra smokes.

Rejoining the Mex for the moment he explained, "I'll be up on the rim in the infernal hot sun whilst you're down here having fun in the shade. When you hit water, dig a few scoops deeper to make sure. Then come up and tell me. Don't holler. If I was sure it was safe to yodel in these hills I wouldn't be setting up a lookout, see?"

Moreno grumbled that he knew how to dig for *agua chingado.* So they parted as friendly as the situation called for and Longarm climbed the north slope of their little canyon. He'd been right about the sunshine up there. But it worked both ways. If the rolling desert between canyon rims offered little shade, it was as grudging about cover for approaching dangers. He figured either *rurales* trailing him and Moreno or *federales* trailing Yaqui would be riding from the northeast. So that was the direction to watch hardest. Yaqui never *let* you watch 'em as they were moving in on you. He could only hope any Yaqui in these parts were more concerned with that army column he and Moreno agreed they might have spotted the night before. So he moved to such shade as there was up there, crawling the last few yards to work his way under a cholla or tree cactus without getting pricked.

Most other cacti were content with stabbing you. The notorious cholla worked more like a small spreading fruit tree covered with fuzzy gray-green eggs instead of leaves. Each was a combined cactus pad and dirty trick. What seemed to be white fuzz sprouting from the greener core worked more like porcupine quills. So even one bitty needle could stick you good and stay stuck 'til you flinched away. Then the whole damned pad, or cholla, busted loose to come along with you, its dead weight driving other needles, lots of other needles, into you.

Critters were driven half loco by cholla. Humans, thinking they were smarter, generally tried to scrape the fuzz-ball off and that part wasn't all that hard. The hard part came later, once the many bitty points driven in too deep to see without a hand lens commenced to fester. There were cases of victims lost and chollad on the desert just blowing out their own brains to get it over with.

Longarm wasn't out to get in that much trouble. Cholla made good cover, if you knew how to cover in it, for the simple reason that even Indians liked to ride *around* the nasty shit.

There were no fuzzy pads against the trunk or even the inner lengths of the lower branches. So once he'd avoided the waist-high outer defenses Longarm was able to sit upright, cross-legged with the Winchester across his lap, and even light a smoke nobody at any distance was likely to notice as some wafted up among the fuzzy gray-green chollas shading him.

He, on the other hand, could see for miles across the shimmering, mostly barren wastes to the Sierra Madres rising lavender-gray over to the northeast. La Sierra Madre Occidental was what Mexicans called the Rockies this far south because they didn't know no better. Sierra meant "saw" or "sawlike" in Spanish and that was a fair description of the Sierra Nevada or Snowy Saw up California way, for the Sierra Nevada was in fact a swamping slab of rock as tilted up, saw-toothed in almost one big piece. But the Sierra Madres, like their rocky sisters to the north, were way more complex. Describing 'em as a herringbone with countless smaller ridges running out from the main spine would be an overly *simple* way of putting it. Longarm preferred to think of the bumpy spine of North America as a whole mess of herrings who'd been migrating more or less north or south when something awful had happened to 'em. He conceded the main continental divide zigged and zagged from Panama to Alaska more or less where they had it on the map. But he knew rival ridges, personal, running off at cockeyed angles, higher than the official central crest.

As if that hadn't been enough to get folk lost, the winding Continental Divide didn't just rise from flat lowlands like the Sierra Nevada or Blue Ridge, back East. North America got to rise some in its own right before its bones commenced to show. That was how come you were a mile high in the sky on the prairie around Denver as you admired what seemed to be the front range of the Rockies off to the west of town.

These gentler swells rose and fell as complicated as the more dramatic peaks looked. As he sat there smoking in the shade of that cholla Longarm wasn't surprised to see most everything to his north, but the distant mountains lay somewhat lower. The canyon behind him ran east to west where they were but had to curve north fairly soon to join the drainage into Arizona Territory. For that was the only way rainwater could run this far north. Longarm knew it would all want to run south, once he and Moreno had worked their way over this almost undetectable and miles-wide rise. Somewhere in the infernal middle, where no serious erosion barred progress east or west, lay the unmapped and likely unmarked Devil's Highway they were looking for.

That rail line just north of the border still followed the best route from the upper Rio Grande to the head of the Sea of Cortez, from whence it was a reasonable haul to more sensible places such as Mission San Diego or Pueblo de Los Angeles in Southern California. But in Spanish Colonial days the best way to haul a wagon hadn't been the best way to cross that sort of Indian Country *alive*.

Ferocious Comanche had made the plains east of El Paso a piss poor place to wander without a cavalry escort, a big cavalry escort. If that hadn't been enough to discourage a heap of Mexicans, the trip was just getting interesting once you'd made her through El Paso.

For if anyone with a lick of sense could see the east-west Mesilla Valley and Hachita Pass through Apacharia was a swell way to run wagon traces and railroads, the Apache could see it better. So the trail even Mexicans used *these* days had had to wait on the civilizing influence of el gringo, white or black, such as, for example, the colored troopers of the 10th U. S. Cavalry, who seemed to scare the Apaches shitless.

Assuming they ever found it, amid all this cactus and stickerbrush, the old-time Spanish had found it safer to follow El Camino Diablo as it wound across high and dry desert between the headwaters of, say, the San Pedro and Santa Cruz running north into the Gila, and the Sonora running into the Sea of Cortez well south of anywhere Longarm was about to show up with a prisoner.

"I need us a guide, or at least a damned map," Longarm announced to a whiptail lizard regarding him cautiously from a nearby pile of windblow. Having confirmed the odd addition to its tiny world was alive, the whiptail whipped back out of sight. Longarm chuckled and consulted his watch. Come eleven or so it would be safe to roll over the rim and see how Moreno was coming with that water in a way more shady part of the world. For not even a Yaqui would be moving across the desert worth mention between, say, eleven and three or four.

Before it got that hot Longarm crawled back out in the sun so he could rise to full height for a serious look. It was surprising how much farther he could see, just standing. He didn't see anything to worry about as he gazed across the shimmering series of gentle rolls to their northeast. But he knew how easy it was to hide whole camps below the skyline in what seemed almost flat prairie. Indians did it all the time. He strode north a few yards from the canyon rim and turned to see how noticeable the tops of those fan palms were, now that the sun was higher.

He was pleased to see they looked more like waist-high chaparral sprouting from level ground than they had at dawn, when the human eye took in shapes more than colors. Despite being distant kin to coconuts and such, desert fan palms grew that same silvery gray as half the thirsty shrubbery in these parts.

So how come he'd just spotted a flash of scarlet red, and there went a twinkle of canary yellow, amid the fronds of one fool palm top!

Longarm eased sideways to view the birds in the treetop or whatever from a different vantage point. Once he had, he saw they didn't have mighty flashy birds in this part of the desert after all. Way off to the south, mayhaps half a mile the other side of that palm top he thought they were bobbing about in, strode a pair of Mex or more likely Pima ladies in white cotton tunics and flouncy skirts of trade sateen, one red and the other yellow. Both gals were packing big straw baskets on their backs, like knapsacks, and both were helping themselves along with long walking, or fruit picking, staffs. They were both walking fast. Longarm knew right off where they had to be going. He moved again to get a palm top between himself and their likely sharp eyes before he strode swiftly to the rim and slid down the north wall on his heels and rump, Winchester serving as a balancing staff. At the bottom he located the ponies and his prisoner in the confusion of deep shade and dazzling sunlight. Moreno was hunkered against a palm trunk near his well. As Longarm approached, the young Mex glanced up, nodded, and said, "We got plenty of water, now. Was only chest deep. I already gave some to *los caballos* and refilled our canteens."

Longarm said, "*Bueno.* Now I got to put the cuffs or leg irons on you for a few minutes, at least. Where would you like to be chained up, old son?"

Moreno scowled and replied, "*Que pesado,* I have done nothing for to deserve such cruelty!"

Longarm explained, "I ain't being cruel. I'm being cautious. We got company heading our way. Looks like Indian gals out to gather some palm fruit from this very canyon. I only got two eyes and three guns to work with. So if it's all the same with you . . ."

"Pendejo, I would rather you just shoot me than to let me fall into Yaqui hands alive, in chains!"

Longarm said, "Don't get your bowels in an uproar. I'm pretty sure they're Pima or Papago and even if they ain't, they're only gals."

He reached for the cuffs with his free hand, adding, "Come on, we want to find something skinnier than a palm if you want me to leave you with your knife hand free."

Moreno said some dreadful things about Longarm's parents, both of 'em, before Longarm had him securely cuffed to desert willow with plenty of shade and water. As he started to turn away, Moreno sort of sobbed, "What if something happens to you? I could die here, *muy lento,* if you failed for to return!"

Longarm said, "That's why I left you your knife. Don't you go to whittling on that willow in less'n say two hours, though. No way you could whittle through in less time than that and I'll be mighty vexed with you if I catch you trying to escape before I was gone long enough to matter, hear?"

Moreno regarded the stout little tree he was cuffed to with distaste as he decided, *"Mierda,* this thirsty *cabrón* is older and tougher than it looks. Would take me all night and then what would I do out here in the middle of nowhere, eh?"

Longarm shrugged and said, "Won't be my problem if I never come back. I got to go round up them other suspicious characters, now."

He did. One of them screamed and fell to her knees, begging for mercy, when Longarm stepped around some cholla on the south rim of the canyon to call out, *"Buendías, muchachas. Estoy policía Americano."*

The prettier one hitched up her yellow skirts, squatted low, and proceeded to scoop dust and desert grits up into her own crotch as she snarled, sloe eyes blazing, *"Vete pa'l carajo,* gringo!"

They were Indian, all right. Longarm chuckled fondly at the memory of the first pretty Paiute gal who'd ever shown him that trick. They'd had a hell of a time getting her old ring-dang-do fit for human consumption again, once she'd decided she liked him after all.

He assured these two, in Spanish, "To repeat my foolish self I am not the sort of gringo you seem to have in mind. I am on my way to my own country with a prisoner. You don't have to worry about *him* raping either of you, either. We have camped in the palm canyon you must have been headed with such big baskets and long poles. As you guessed, the palm fruit is ripe and you should be happy to hear no other Ho have beaten you to it."

The one who'd been just ruining her own privates stopped scooping up grits as she shot him a wary look and a long string of Nahuatloid at him. When he laughingly protested he was only a *saltu* she demanded, in Spanish, "How is it you know our word for People, then? Those of you with any manners at all call us Pima. I do not know for why some call us Cavaros. We do not dig in the soil half as much as the peones *Español* who call us that."

Longarm nodded soberly and said, "Some Ho of the Great Basin to the north dig enough desert roots and bulbs to qualify for the name. But since I see you're here for palm fruit why don't we all go down where it's much cooler. We've tobacco as well as water to share with you after that long walk you've both had from . . . Where did you say you came from with those baskets?"

The plumper one in the red skirt might have told him. The pretty one who'd just ruined herself for any other fun snapped, "We did not say!" as she got back to her feet, giving her companion a warning glare.

Longarm decided he liked her, despite her dusty and doubtless downright painful *cosita*. A man just had to admire a spunksome little thing who put her own moral notions ahead of her own life, some men taking that literally dirty trick more serious than him, and of course she was obviously thinking more of the safety of her own people than getting on the good side of a well-armed stranger, or *saltu*, as one said in most of the Uto-Aztec dialects of the Ho.

He let them slide down into the canyon ahead of him, lest they suffer heat stroke lighting out across the open desert the moment he gave them such a swell lead on his rifle.

Neither let on how thirsty they'd really gotten as he watered them both with separate canteens near the well he'd had Moreno dig in that big shady patch. Longarm could see they'd been out in that sun longer than planned by the amount of dainty sips they took.

Watching from where he was keeping such close company with that distant willow, Moreno called out in English, "Hey, don't I get for to join the party, you selfish *cabrón?*"

Longarm laughed, called back, "Hold the thought. It's too early to say," before he turned back to the Pima girls to explain, "He is the prisoner I told you about. You don't have to worry about either of us. We are only going to be here until it cools enough to ride on. It is not for me to tell Ho how to gather desert fruits. But if I only had two baskets to fill I think I would wait until there was a little more shade and pole the bunches down a few at a time. I wouldn't even consider carrying a full load back across the open desert, on foot, before nightfall."

The one in the yellow skirts, who seemed to speak for both of them friendly or not, said, "That is the way we planned our visit here. We spent too much of last night in another patch of shade and that is for why the sun caught us out in the open this morning like *cucarachas* lost on a baking tortilla."

He said he hadn't taken them for Mex kids who might have strayed from a wagon train and handed each a slim brown cheroot.

They both seemed to admire three-for-a-nickel smokes and of course he was honoring Indian women by offering to smoke with 'em. He'd long since learned it was less work to honor Indians than it was to fight 'em. Over by that willow Moreno called out, "Hey, what about me?" and so Longarm explained, in English, "We're running low and I'd rather be rude to you than them. You don't seem to know your way on this desert any better than I do. These gals live hereabouts.

So hush and let me see if I can find out where in thunder we are."

Someone else was asking, *"Que hora es?"* So he fished out his watch—they seemed to admire that as well—and announced it would soon be high noon.

The Pima gals chatted some about that in their own twittersome lingo. Then the pretty one with the yellow skirts and gritty crotch said, "We thought it was getting that hot. After we finish this fine tobacco and drink some more water we wish for to sleep a little. It feels better to sleep naked, wrapped in canvas, than on the sand as if one was an animal. How do you feel about this?"

Longarm took a thoughtful drag on his cheroot, knowing how easy it was to get mixed up talking Spanish to a lady who likely thought in Nahuatl. He decided, "We have two bedrolls and I don't see why you *muchachas* couldn't use them both to catch up on your beauty rest until it's time for my prisoner and me to ride on."

She said, *"Bueno.* Which one of us gets to turn in with you and who gets stuck with that handsome but sort of fresh mestizo?"

Longarm blinked in not displeased surprise. They were both nicely built if a man liked 'em short and chunky. The more forward of the two was way prettier. On the other hand a man had to study on where he might want to shove his poor old organ grinder and he'd seen her scoop at least a sugar-scoop worth of dusty grit where it could really do a heap of damage to a poor passionate cuss.

He could see how much he really had to say about it when the two of 'em compared some more notes in their own bird tweets and the moon-faced gal in the red skirts pouted like a loser and stared sulky in Moreno's general direction. They both laughed, however, when the bolder one made a suggestion that sounded lewd whether one savvied their lingo or not. When the pretty one said she was called something he could only recall as Shitty Tits he asked if she didn't have a mission name. She said, "We are free Ho, not mission peons. *Pero* some of the Ho boys call me something ruder that translates into Spanish more delicately as Zorrita."

He decided he'd call her Rita, lest he slip up, for he'd already guessed how Ho boys might mean what translated literal as Little Bitch-Fox. Most Indian dialects described things way more exactly than English or Spanish could, with separate words for say a fox standing up, a fox laying down, a fox after a chicken or out to get laid. Miss Shitty Tits, or Rita, was mighty bold for a Pima or even a Mex gal. Indians who hadn't been messed up by missionaries had a nice clean attitude toward good, clean fun. But they still expected at least a little flirting and nose-flute serenading, first, as a rule.

To give himself time to figure, Longarm rose, ambled over to the piled saddles, and unlashed Moreno's bedroll first. As he carried it over to his prisoner, along with a canteen Moreno might wind up wanting as well, the one he'd called Rita seemed to be tagging along. When he dropped the canteen and bedroll by Moreno she said, "Oh, I thought you meant us."

She'd said it in Spanish, so Moreno made kissing noises with his lips as he told her, "Don't go for *him, chiquita! La via es breve* and I eat it better than any gringo!"

She sniffed and replied, "*Pero* you are still an ugly *mestizo* who could use a bath, no?"

Moreno growled, "*Chingate!*"

To which she demurely replied, "I do not have to. I have this tall *caballero* to do it *for* me!"

Then she called her friend over to help Moreno out as she took Longarm's elbow with her free hand, pointed up the canyon with her fruit pole, and suggested they leave the two lovebirds in privacy.

Longarm didn't want anyone thinking he was a spoilsport. He wanted the Pima gals to help him find El Camino Diablo more than he wanted a gritty dick. But little Rita sure seemed to make her mind up sudden and act accordingly. Had he not seen her taking the standard Indian precautions against casual sex he'd have sworn she was out to seduce him for some ulterior motives of her own.

He picked up his own bedroll along the way but advised her, as they walked arm in arm up the shady canyon, "This Winchester *Americano* fires fifteen times without reloading. But you did say your Ho band was far from here, didn't you?"

She sighed and said, "Two days, alas, on foot. The old ones told us we might regret going so far after palm fruit this late in the hot moons, *pero* all the fresh fruit had been gathered within an easy distance and I have always been cursed by what my people call, let me see, a tooth that is too sweet?"

He said he followed her drift and pointed up at a heavily laden fan palm, saying, "You'll fill that basket you're packing easy enough. But wouldn't you say you and your friend will be carrying more semisweet water than anything else as you head for home?"

She wrinkled her nose and said, "*Sí, pero* I *like* my fruit fresh and juicy. I know tunas, *pitahayas y acebos*, keep better and taste sweeter once they have been pulped and sun dried. *Pero*, I don't know, something seems to be missing."

Before he could answer they'd come upon a shady patch of spring-sprouted and summer-cured love grass and she seemed to like that a heap as well. So he spread the roll for them atop the vanilla-scented straw and only then remembered the tin of rubber contraceptives he'd been packing in one saddlebag ever since he'd parted from that overly superstitious schoolmarm up Trinity way. As a rule, as he'd warned that schoolmarm, using a rubber spoiled half the fun. But on the other hand, that sweet little thing teaching school in Trinity hadn't made a habit of stuffing her snatch with bird cage gravel!

He was trying to come up with a polite excuse for going back for some protection when he noticed how fast one could shuck the basic Pima outfit. As she tossed her basket and loose cotton tunic one way, the sateen skirt the other, and threw herself down atop the bedding with a right inviting smile, Longarm figured he'd best at least assure her of his friendly intent. So he got rid of his hat, vest, and gun rig to flop down beside her. Before he could do anything else she was all over him, pleading, "*Acostarnos y meter mano, por favor!*"

So, seeing she'd asked polite, Longarm stretched them both out flat and proceeded to finger her as requested, figuring his work-toughened hands could take at least as much abuse as her dusty *cosita*. But then, once he had a firm grip on the subject, he discovered her innards felt more like warm custard than the moist sand he'd been braced for.

He laughed and called her a sneaky little sleight-of-hand artist in English. She asked what he'd said and he just told her she was beautiful. He'd seldom met a woman who wanted to hear anything else at a time like this.

He knew he was right when she sobbed, "*Ay, Madre de Dios,* stop teasing me and *meter el todo, amante mío!*"

So he did, and she helped him undress himself atop her as they both bumped and ground until the musky odors of human lust mingled with that of love grass straw pounded to sweet-smelling chaff. She said she liked it even better with both of them stark and her on top.

He had no complaints as she bounced her tawny torso skillsome on her chunky brown thighs. For there was a heap to be said for Indian seating arrangements, and he'd seldom met a gal raised Indian who couldn't squat and bounce, like so, indefinite. No white gal he'd told about it had ever managed, experimenting, to come the way some Indian gals could, hunkered low with a heel tendon rubbing them the right way down yonder. When he asked this one, Rita giggled and said she preferred bouncing on such a *pitón grande*. So he knew she masturbated that way when she had to and likely did so picturing just what she was doing with his shaft instead. He knew he was right when she cupped her bare breasts in both hands, closed her eyes, and crooned in her own lingo with a dreamy smile, as if she was all alone with the dong of her dreams. So he closed his own eyes and tried to convince himself he was in a fancy four-poster with someone pretty and high-toned as Miss Ellen Terry of the London Stage and Police Gazette. He sure admired *that* lovely lady's looks, but it hardly seemed likely a lady who acted Shakespeare, even in tights, would bite down that hard with her love-slicked innards. So he decided she was mayhaps that redheaded Princess of Wales instead and fired a handsome salute up Her Highness as she suddenly moaned, *"Ay, alma de mi corazón, venirte en mi higado!"*

They both knew it wasn't half as deep as her liver and never would be. But he did his best to shove it up her that far, even knowing she was shitting him a mite, seeing she'd switched back to Spanish and had to have more control of her feelings, now.

Of course, that worked out nice for him, since no gal screwed like a gal who was out to please her partner more than herself. He rolled her over on her back to finish right with her bare ankles locked across the nape of his neck and it was easy to feed her the same romantic shit as he pounded them both to glory again.

He'd told other more suspicious gals in the past that it wasn't fair to accuse a man of fibbing when he sweet-talked a gal he was coming in. Most men really meant what they were saying, at the time they were saying it. For it was almost impossible to get that friendly with a gal without feeling, well, mighty friendly.

He knew he was making her feel swell, too, when she switched back to her Indian dialect and commenced to move her hips under him as if she had a hardrock miner's steam drill stuck in her tailbone.

Once they had to stop, as all critters mortal, dammit, had to in time, Rita snuggled close, murmuring, *"Ay, que rapto supremo* and are you ashamed, now, you proud gringo?"

He asked what in thunder he had to feel ashamed of, knowing how much that might please her. He knew it had when she said, "Some Mexicans who wish for to be taken for *blancopuro* seem to feel they have lowered themselves after they have made love to a mere India, or even a mestiza, no?"

He patted her love-flushed bare shoulder and assured her, "I wouldn't know about stuck-up Mexicans. I avoid such feelings by never kissing anyone I don't have any respect for."

For some reason that got her to crying. She sobbed, "*Ay, mierda,* I was going to ask a favor and now you shall think me a *puta* who only makes love when she *wants* something, no?"

He said, "No. Everyone gets something when they make love. We call it coming, in English, when we *venir.* What else were you going to ask me to do for you, or with you, once I get my second wind."

She shyly suggested, "Is a long way back to our *rancharita* and you were right about how heavy fresh fruit can be."

He chuckled and replied, "*Por supuesto,* we have four *caballos* and neither of you *muchachas* weigh as much as an *hombre,* even with a basket of palm fruit."

"You will not say I only *chinga* for to get a ride home?" she insisted, now that she'd already done it.

He soothed, "I'm not going to say I kissed you in front of any of your people. As for who might be taking advantage of whom, I was about to ask you and your friend to guide us as far west as El Camino Diablo, if that is what your own people call it."

She brightened and said, "*Pero* no. We *respect* this dry gathering ground but we do not *fear* it enough to say it belongs to the evil one of your religion. If you speak of a route all the way west to the great bitter water we can not promise you that much. *Pero* we do know of trails, connected trails, the Spanish black robes used in the grandfather times. Only wicked Mexicans and *los rurales* who hunt them ride that way, these days."

He nodded and said, "That sounds like El Camino Diablo, all right."

Before he could question her further about local geography she called the limp thing she was fondling "*pobrecito*" and shyly asked if he could use an inspiring *"chopa."*

To which he could only reply, *"Sin falta!"* and forget about everything else for a pleasant interlude. For she couldn't have answered the question in any case with her mouth so full.

Further down the canyon, as Rita was going down on Longarm, the handcuffed Moreno was having his own problems in the dappled shade of that willow with the moon-faced little thing he'd decided to call Chiflada. That didn't sound at all like her Pima name. Moreno still would have argued it fit her. Chiflada translates roughly from rude Mexican as Prick Teaser.

She'd stripped to the chunky buff as soon as they'd unrolled the prisoner's own bedding. Getting Moreno out of his boots and pants, despite that wrist cuffed to that tree, had been easy enough. Getting his homespun cotton shirt off hadn't been much tougher. It bunched neatly over the chain between his fist and that tree trunk.

Getting Chiflada to just spread her muscular thighs and *take* it seemed to be the problem. First she demanded he let her get on top, which seemed reasonable. Then she squatted over him and took it to the roots in her pulsating wet *cosita,* which seemed divine. Then, just as he was coming she popped off, swapped ends, and presented her broad brown behind for full close inspection as she demurely demanded they finish *"sesenta y nueve"* which means sixty-nine in any lingo when a couple finds itself in that position.

Juanito Moreno considered himself as good a sport as that other Don Juan. So he gulped, grinned, held his breath for the moment and gingerly stuck out his tongue. He'd learned from experience that once you could stand the smell you had it half-licked and at least it felt marvelous at one's other end.

Most of the time. Women who did it with their lips pursed over their teeth were divine. Women who scraped their damned teeth over one's damned *pitón* were better than nothing, as long as they were careful. Women who *chewed* were simply *aborrecible!*

"Watch those *chingado* teeth!" Moreno moaned, even as he felt himself rising higher to the occasion. It felt as if she was sliding a sliced open cactus pad up and down on it. The feeling was wet, slippery, and thorny. To show her how it felt he sucked in her turgid chocolate clit and bit down on it. She moaned in surprised delight and damned near bit the head off his *piton* as she came in his face in a series of shuddering orgasms.

As she rolled off at last, crooning, *"Ay, que linda!"* Moreno groaned, "Speak for yourself. Even better, finish this off for me. With your *chingado* hand if you're too proud to please an *hombre* in the usual manner."

She yawned and said she was tired. Suiting her actions to her words she rolled on one side with her naked back to Moreno and said something dumb about *la siesta.*

It was, in fact, getting uncomfortably warm for further excitement. But Moreno was already excited, where it mattered most to most men. He stroked it a few times with his free hand. He had to admit that felt a lot better than her cruel fangs. But there was something missing and the Church said playing with oneself was the sure path to hell by way of an insane asylum. So he decided it would be safer to rape her.

Juanito Moreno didn't consider it rape, of course. It could have been argued by many an Anglo college boy that "rape" had to be an oxymoron when applied to a lady who'd already given short shrift with her vagina and a lousy blow job. So Moreno was sincerely surprised by the Pima girl's reaction when he fumbled for that knife among his discarded garments, gripped the blade between his bared teeth, and rolled her back where he wanted her, spread-eagle, to hiss as he mounted her, "Just hold still and let me do it my way or by the balls of El Cristo I shall slit your *chingado* throat and cut off your *chupas!"*

She screamed, loudly, but didn't otherwise resist as he entered her. So Moreno was humping her hot and heavy a few moments later when Longarm suddenly loomed over them, naked as a jay but .44-40 in hand, to demand, "Cut that out, Moreno!"

When his passionate prisoner did no such thing Longarm warned, "I'd sure hate to blow a man's ass off when it was bouncing so comical, but that gal you're bouncing in claims loud and clear she's being raped!"

"Is that what she's been yelling about in Pima?" laughed Moreno, getting in some more good thrusts as Longarm sighed and said, "Aw, cut that out, old son. I can see the way she's moving, too. But I still have it on good authority she wants you to stop!"

As if to back his word the prettier Pima called Rita appeared on the scene, modestly concealing most of her charms behind the yellow skirting she was holding down her front side, at least. She trilled in their own dialect to Chiflada, who trilled back, pouty but sort of passionate as Moreno went on banging her.

Rita told Longarm, "She says he goes too deep, *pero* not fast enough, and that she has promised her own Pima lover she would never carry flirtation with another man all the way."

Moreno, overhearing, sobbed, "Jesus, Maria y Jose the teasing *cochina* just gave me a French lesson, *pero* a bad one, and if I do not finish right I am going to die right here!"

Longarm found the way the plump one was moving her chunky hips more convincing than his prisoner's words. He turned to the one with him and muttered, "They're both acting stupid. Race you back to *our* place?"

She thought that a grand notion, so in the end, a grand time was had by all.

Chapter 6

By late afternoon it got cool enough for more serious work with one's clothes on. Moreno said he was willing to help the gals pick palm fruit. But Longarm had a safer if less pleasant chore for him. Having noticed how filled with surprises the young Mex seemed to be, Longarm took him up on the rim, along with the leg irons Marshal Vail had insisted he carry along, and had Moreno sit in the lengthening shade of that same cholla with a tall saguaro cactus between his leather-clad calves. Then he chained the prisoner's ankles together and handed him his derringer again, saying, "Lay flat on your back and fire straight up so's the sound'll carry if you spy anything important coming. The gals say they doubt anyone will be. They come out this way with privacy in mind as they gathered fresh fruit."

"*Chinga las Pimas,* how am I supposed to run for it if a war band of Yaqui or even that army column is coming this way?"

Longarm regarded the tall, skinny saguaro looming high above them with three J-shaped arms making a mockery of his words as he suggested, "I reckon you could shinny up and off if you don't care about thorns in your palms and balls. Warn the rest of us in time and I'll be up here with my Winchester and the key to them leg irons before anyone can reach you from the far horizon."

Moreno insisted he was a heartless bastard, if not an actual Protestant who ate his mother on a Friday as Longarm ambled back to tend his own chores while the Pima gals filled their big baskets. Once he had everything else they'd be packing along aboard the four ponies, he left his Winchester in its saddle boot, found his own pole, and pitched in to help them knock down bunches they were having the hardest times with. Rita was all for spending the coming night there. Chiflada said they might as well, now that she'd never be able to face her true love again. But Longarm was anxious to get an early start on any night-riding Yaqui. When Rita pointed it out to him that Yaqui seldom moved out of camp before pitch blackness on a moonless night, Longarm told her that was what he'd just said.

Knocking down a big squishy bunch of ripe black fruit he added, "I doubt Yaqui will want to stray even this far from the foothills of their Sierra Madre hunting grounds. I'd still like a few more dry and dusty *varas* of your Ho country between us and the hills by owlhoot time."

So they all got back to work and filled the blamed baskets to overflowing. The most practical way to load a Pima gal and a Pima gathering basket aboard a pony was to have her strap it on her back and then fork her aboard the pony. The one Moreno had dubbed Chiflada had more trouble and needed more help. He saw what Moreno meant when he found his helping hand so deep in her crack, as surprised as he was. But once he had her aboard she looked as if butter wouldn't melt in her mouth as she thanked him, demure and innocent as anything.

He took his Winchester with him as he climbed back up to fetch Moreno. As he was taking his leg irons and derringer back, his prisoner asked if he'd really considered the wisdom of leaving four ponies in the care of two Indians of any nation or gender. Longarm soothed, "That's how come I hung on to this saddle gun. Ain't no pony can outrun a rifle-ball on open desert, and I suspect Chiflada likes you more than she lets on in any case."

As if to prove him right they found both Indian maids and the other stock right where he'd left them. He made sure all the canteens were filled and that everyone's bladder was empty before he got back in his McClellan, shoved the Winchester back in its boot, and announced, *"Vamanos pa'l carajo!"*

So they did. The canyon forked the wrong way once they'd followed it some to the west. So he found a side gully that led to the top, and once they were riding abreast across open desert again it was easier to see why it was covered with such scrawny stickerbrush and scrawny cactus. The Sonora sun was a pure bitch in August, even when it was low in the western sky. For while the shadows it was casting covered more of the baked desert pavement, the glare getting through was smacking them full in their faces. Neither man's hat brim did a lick of good and of course neither gal had started out with hat-one.

Being desert Indians, they were content with telling Longarm he was *idioso* to ride right into the sun when he could be having much more fun in the shade. Moreno was as worried about Yaqui or worse than Longarm. So he was content to growl, *"Este chingado calor me va a matar!"* and then add in English, lest Longarm failed to grasp his meaning, "This fucking heat is going to kill me!"

Longarm growled back, *"Cierra el hocico,* meaning shut your trap, and you never had it so good. I swear my boss, Marshal Billy Vail, will have a fit if he ever finds out I've been hauling federal prisoners through Old Mexico and getting them laid."

He'd kept his first few words of English teasing and light lest the Pima gals worry about what they were talking about. Once he had the bilingual Mex joshing back as casual he said, lightly, "Speaking of laying ladies whose menfolk can feel just as proddy about it as two Mex brothers and her father, we're going to have to study on just how close to their own kin we want to drop these gals off."

Moreno shrugged and said, "Is no problem, now. I got mine eating out of my hand, with her *chingado* teeth under control, now that I have made her come my way, more than once."

Longarm still seemed dubious. Moreno tried, "Whether she really loves me as much as she says she does or not, can you see a *muchacha* telling her own *hombres* she gave her all to another none of them even knew?"

Longarm sighed and said, "Yep. First time it happened to me her name was Ramona or mayhaps Felicidad. I only remember the details of the fight that ensued out back as I was escorting her home."

The young but worldly border Mex chuckled and said, "Ay, que *nalgason,* you gringo assholes are always falling for that one. *Muchachos* who lay for an *hombre* with shoes who has been set up by one of their *putas* do not really care what you have been doing to her. They are after the *shoes,* no matter what she has told them. If she really meant anything to even one of them, and she told them she had gone all the way . . ."

"I know how romance works down this way," Longarm cut in, switching back to Spanish to tell Moreno the sun was good for his pimples when he noticed the way Rita was frowning, back yonder.

Twisting in his saddle, he called back, in Spanish, "It will soon be dark and you were right about the moon rising late the past few nights. I want you to think about shade and water ahead. Meanwhile, are there any dangers I should be thinking about if we push on a few *varas* after sunset?"

She said, "Not before almost midnight, at the pace you are setting, and by then the moon should be up. The mesquite-shaded arroyo we sheltered in the night before we met you is over to the south a good bit. Should we continue straight, there is an old Spanish ruin. Was where the black robes changed teams and sheltered from the sun in the grandfather times, I have been told. Some say there is still water there. I know there are trees. The black robes knew that if you watered trees by hand, a lot, they could sink their roots in time to the water that is always there, near the bedrock."

She thought harder and added, "The trees there are only good for shade, I think. I would have heard if any bore fruit or nuts a mouse would care about."

He said he didn't doubt that. He'd already noticed Ho et fruits and nuts he'd have never bothered feeding to a pet mouse. Some, he had to allow, were only odd to whites because whites had simply never heard of 'em and didn't expect to find anything worth a chaw out where even the buzzards looked half starved.

Most whites who tried 'em had to allow tunas, off prickle pear, pitaya, off the tall saguaro, and even the cloying sugar substitute made from gound mesquite pods tasted better than nothing. Indians and even some Mex peons, having less to choose from, tended to gather food, fiber, and beverages from less likely sources. It had been Marshal Vail, a former Texas Ranger, who'd pointed out how the first cuss who'd ever made liquor out of a wormy old mescal or century plant, likely some desperate Aztec, had surely hankered to get drunk. Longarm knew Papago bothered with the bitty black seeds of Red Maidens, a desert *portulaca,* which tasted all right once ground to a flour that looked like black gunpowder, but, Kee-rist, what a heap of *effort* for such modest *results!*

It seemed to take forever. But at last the sun went down, the stars came out, and some sweet-smelling desert flowers commenced to attract bats from all over. The fluttering was annoying but only dangerous when it spooked a pony. Ponies could be as silly about bats as Eastern schoolmarms or lonesome Denver widows. Longarm had to smile as he recalled that time he'd had to save that hystericated widow woman from a bat who'd wound up in her bedroom and was aiming to get tangled in her hair or fly up under her nightgown, she felt sure. They never would have gotten rid of that bat if she hadn't let him trim her lamp, take down her hair, and make sure it wasn't under her nightgown after all.

He wondered why he was thinking about that friendly old gal just now. He'd been enjoying another one all afternoon, the sun was barely down, and Rita said they'd be stopping at those ruins in a little while.

He wanted another smoke, too. He told himself he couldn't have one, dammit. Aside from being almost out of cheroots, he was way up in the middle of the air and the flare of a match could be seen a good five miles in dry desert air after dark.

That reminded him to twist in the saddle and stare back the way they'd come. He couldn't even make out his three companions in the bat fluttery gloom near the ground. Up above, of course, the desert stars hung so bright and looked so close he was tempted to stand in the stirrups and see how many he could scoop from the sky in his hat.

He never, of course. Aside from reading *Scientific American* when he came across a copy he didn't have to pay for, he had no idea what he'd do with a star if he ever caught one.

The wind perked up long before the moon did. Longarm was tempted to break out his frock coat and put it on over his buttoned-up vest. He didn't want his more lightly clad companions to think him a sissy. So he just put up with the shivering as they rode on. Natives of this part of the world got used to feeling half fried and half froze within most any twenty-four-hour period. They got to feel comfortable when things got sort of in between, and there was a lot to be said for early morns and late afternoons or early evenings in these parts. That was when Mexicans and their Indian cousins got things done. So it wasn't fair to dismiss a lazy-looking Mex dozing off in broad day as what he looked like until you'd seen him chopping cotton at a time most Anglos were still slugabed, or dancing the fandango and fighting some gal's brother, ferocious, long after folk in cooler climes had called it a day.

By midnight that night, though, the open desert had gotten cold as a banker's heart, and even the Pima gals were bitching about it. Longarm reined in and had everyone dismount while he broke out some blankets. After they'd watered the ponies, they remounted and rode on. Moreno and the two gals assured him he was a saint and he didn't feel as guilty with his frock coat on, buttoned snug.

Moreno said he'd been thinking about buying a gringo outfit, as soon as he figured what one did with all that stuffy *mierda* when it wasn't cold, which was more than half the time in more civilized parts of his country.

Longarm chuckled and said, "We've never figured it, neither. There's this song we sung in school about polar bears living where no summers occur and the rest of the time wrapped up in polar bear fur while . . . Now how did the rest of that go?"

He thought, then began to sing in a pleasant enough baritone:

"'We poor unfortunates live in a clime,
As calls for at least three full suits at a time.
A thick one and a thin one for the days cold and hot,
And a medium weight suit for the days that are not.'"

Moreno laughed. The Pima girls didn't get it but asked him to sing some more. He said he was tempted but added, "Voices carry out this way at night. I shouldn't have done that in the first place."

They started singing, anyway. Fortunately Indian singing tended to be soft as well as monotonous. Indians spoke lots of different lingo, held all sorts of religious notions, and nobody could ever say an easygoing Pueblo had much in common with say a Comanche or Lakota, yet they'd all apparently been to the same music school, way back when. Indian singing always reminded Longarm of what the tone-deaf U. S. Grant had said about his own taste in music. He'd allowed he only knew two songs. One was Yankee Doodle and the other wasn't.

They commenced to get on his nerves after an hour or more of chanting the same words over and over again. But when Moreno yelled at them to shut up Longarm growled, "Leave 'em be. They're a long way from home and likely as worried as we are."

"*Mierda,* who is worried?" asked Moreno.

To which Longarm could only reply, "*Now* who's talking like a total asshole?"

The moon rose at last, painting everything around them the same shade of tarnished pewter. As ever on open plains or desert, it looked as if they hadn't ridden far enough to matter. As an experienced rider, Longarm had been keeping a rough tally on their hoofbeats, resting the ponies every five or six miles, so he wasn't too surprised when they topped a gentle rise to spy something big and shapeless crouching on the starry skyline up ahead.

Rita called out, "*Mirate,* is those ruins I told you about, no?"

Longarm decided, "That or the biggest damn clump of tumbleweed this child's ever seen. You three stay here while I move in to scout it."

The gals protested that none of their own people ever bothered with the roofless ruins and worthless trees. Moreno swore softly and said, "He is not worried about Pima, or even Papago," as Longarm rode on, hauling his Winchester from its boot and levering a round in the chamber.

He moved in to where he could just make out the paler ghostly forms of 'dobe walls against the inky lace outlines of the trees they surrounded. Then he reined in, dismounted, tethered his pony to some chamisbrush, and crabbed sideways through the mostly waist-high chaparral to spiral in, ready to hit the dirt, with his saddle gun trained on the ruins from his hip.

Nobody seemed to care. After he'd rolled over a low windowsill to land in a cautious crouch in one corner of the layout, he saw he was covering mayhaps an acre and a half of bare dirt dappled by moonlight and dotted with a confusion of contorted gnomish trees.

He double-checked, poking around some blind corners and behind the thicker tree trunks. None were all that thick. The old timers who must have had a roof and at least some furniture, long ago, had planted cork oaks and *palo verdes* out front, on the south side, for shade. Once the shade was considerable and the roofing had caved in, or been carried off as salvage, smaller volunteers had sprouted inside the shell, where, aside from shade and some shelter from the drying winds, they likely got watered better after a rare desert shower. It was easy to see there was no way for rainwater to run once it landed inside the shells of the abandoned buildings and surrounding garden walls.

Some of the younger saplings seemed to be mesquite and ironwood, by moonlight, leastways. Desert critters had likely dropped their seeds in a better than average place at the right time of the desert year. Longarm knew both species bore seed pods worth at least a Ho food gatherer's time. But mayhaps nobody from Rita's band had been up this way, recent.

Somebody had. He'd stepped in fairly fresh horse shit before he noticed all the moonlit pebbles and cobbles in these parts might not be solid rock, after all.

He wiped his feet as best he could on a patch of creeping sedum spread like a doormat across a break in the east wall. Then he ambled out to where he'd tethered his mount and rode part way back to the others. They naturally rode to join him. Once they had he said, "Nobody there, now. Somebody else rode through no more than forty-eight hours ago and possibly less. Do your *hombres* hunt on horseback, Rita?"

She said her band had a few burros as well as the usual goats and free-ranging chickens but added, "My people are not too ignorant for to keep *caballos*. Our country is simply not rich enough for to feed anything that eats so much and does so little."

Longarm nodded. He wasn't surprised. Ho speakers included such horse nations as the Comanche and Shoshone, but even white prospectors settled for a pack burro at most in pure desert. He decided the mystery rider or riders who'd passed this way ahead of them were likely Mexicans on their own way across the desert.

"Or Yaqui, out searching for fun," said Moreno in a cheersome tone.

Longarm didn't tell him he was full of it. He knew Yaqui were distant kin to the friendlier Pima and Papago who lived more like their Comanche cousins on the far side of their widespread family tree, save for being even tougher to get along with than Comanche.

Waving his rifle barrel at the ruins ahead he decided, "Whether they're long gone or coming back we'll still be safer forted up in them 'dobe walls, and there won't be any place so cool and shady for miles, once the sun's back up."

They didn't argue. As he led them on in, he continued, "We'll shelter here 'til say three or four and try to get an earlier start, tomorrow. Do you ladies think we'll have you well on your way home by say this time tomorrow night?"

Rita said, "Earlier than that. As I told you before, we are trending north of a direct line to our *rancherita. Pero* is a north-south game trail we should come to before another sunset and our *rancherita* is only a few *veras,* downhill, most of the way."

The dumpier Pima gal asked why they couldn't help them with all their heavy palm fruit, pointing out it would only call for a few hours more.

Longarm didn't answer. He'd been raised polite and there was no polite way to tell an Indian lady why you might not want to drop by her *rancherita,* as Apache camps were also called in these parts.

Pima men were at least as friendly as your average Mex peon, but a stranger dropping a well-screwed señorita off on her daddy's doorstep would be tempting fate as foolishly.

Once inside, the ponies proved he'd been right about some of those saplings being mesquite. As they were unsaddled and tethered among some, near the south wall where they'd catch plenty of shade after sunrise, all four commenced to browse on the feathery leaves and twisty brown pods as if they were in a candy store. The Pima gals confirmed that the less sweet but plumper pods on similar but less spreading branches were full of nutlike ironwood seeds. But they didn't care. They said they were starting to like Longarm's pork and beans way better. As she took Longarm's bedroll from his saddle, unbidden, Rita confided there were lots of things about him a gal could surely get used to.

He still took the first watch, warning Moreno to get at least a few winks of genuine sleep this side of midnight. The young Mex just laughed. The gals seemed sort of put out, judging by the way they bitched back and forth in their own lingo.

Longarm assured Rita of his undying devotion, finished his damned beans, and strode outside the walls with his frock coat on and his saddle gun cradled over an elbow. He chewed a stem of wild anise in place of the smoke he was dying for as he slowly circled the whole layout, half a rifle shot out. It was seldom one got to set up a night picket so scientific. Few night camps were set up as such tempting bullseyes in the center of so much nothing much.

A million years went by as Longarm slowly paced off at least a million miles. At last it was pushing midnight and all he had to show for so much effort was that nobody had butchered them all in their bedrolls. So he drifted in to rouse Moreno.

Longarm was a big man who tipped the scales considerable, but as more than one Indian had commented with admiration, he walked way quieter than most in his low-heeled stove-pipe boots.

Thus it came to pass that Moreno and the naked gal atop the bedding with him were going at it hot and heavy as Longarm materialized above them in the moonlight.

The gal being on the bottom, spied him first and gasped, "*Ay, querido,* let me explain before you do anything cruel!"

Longarm smiled down thinly and softly replied, "I'm not here to be cruel to anyone, Rita. I'm here to post this passionate *cabrón* out on picket. Are you listening to me, you passionate *cabrón?*"

Moreno moaned, "No, I'm coming, or I would be, if you weren't being such a pain in the *culo* about good, clean fun!"

Longarm grimaced and said, "Don't let me stand in your way. Just finish *poco tiempo* and I'll be waiting over by that break in the south wall. Got to take a leak in any case."

Then he turned and left them to their fun, muttering, "All right, when was the last time *you* two-timed a trusting soul and wasn't it fun?"

Then he pissed all over some rabbit bush, pretending it was them, and had his feelings under control by the time Moreno joined him with a sheepish smile and most of his buttons fastened.

The federal prisoner murmured, *"No tengo razón, lo se, pero* was not my idea. She said as long as none of us would ever see one another again . . ."

"I know what she said," Longarm cut in, adding, "I'd have doubtless done the same, in your place." He chuckled and admitted, "Hell, I've done the same in *her* place. Ain't we humans imaginative sinners?"

"Then we are still *amigos?"* tried the prisoner.

To which Longarm was forced to reply, "Let's not get silly about it. I'm still taking you back to Denver and a fate you doubtless deserve. Meanwhile, I can't stay awake around the clock and somebody has to stand watch. I don't see how I can let you run loose out here with even blanks in this derringer. You've got that pig sticker, too, right?"

Moreno confessed he never left his bedroll without it and Longarm decided, *"Bueno,* let's move up the wall to where that ironwood's sprouted through the 'dobe. I'll cuff you to that and you're welcome to whittle ironwood all night for all I care."

Moreno didn't point out that would hardly be enough time. They were starting to understand one another better. Cuffed by his left wrist to the almost uncuttable branch, below a fork, the prisoner was free to stand, squat, or sit in the sedum along the base of the wall. Longarm handed him the derringer, grunting, "You know the way it goes. I'd rather have you further out. But that wouldn't be as fair to you if someone really came pussyfooting in through all that chaparral."

"*Mierditas,* you call *this* fair?" demanded his prisoner with an anxious look around as he pointed out, "I feel like a *chingado* worm on a *chingado* hook, dangled for to catch Yaqui!"

Longarm shrugged and said, "That's about the size of it. I ain't about to arm a prisoner with a more serious weapon. But at least you'll be tougher to get at, here. They might not even notice you if you flatten out before you call out to me with that whore pistol."

Moreno said he was sure he knew where Longarm had learned about whore pistols. But Longarm had chuckled off before his prisoner softly growled, "At your mother's knee, while you were eating her."

Longarm didn't feel up to another dumb conversation with the pretty but perfidious Rita. So he headed direct for his own bedroll. He couldn't see why he was so surprised to find it occupied, as soon as he studied on it.

The one they'd dubbed Chiflada didn't speak half as much Spanish and Longarm spoke even less Ho, but it didn't matter and may have smoothed the way for him. She sure felt smooth as well as tight and hot once he'd simply shucked his duds, rolled under the covers with her to find her jay naked and spread wide so's he simply had to put it in.

If her face wasn't as pretty and her figure was a mite more rounded than old Rita's, she made up for a heap with enthusiasm, and it was hard to fathom why Moreno had been calling her a prick teaser.

It wouldn't have been polite to ask, but later, as they were sharing one of his rare and almost priceless three-for-a-nickels, she confided shyly that while she never did this sort of thing, as a rule, she'd wanted to do it with him instead of that mere peon from the beginning.

He said he was glad and asked whose grand notion it had been to switch playmates this evening. She giggled and said it had been mutual. They'd agreed that since they'd be ruined forever if any of their kith and kin found out they'd stooped to screwing *saltu,* they might as well have all the fun they could with all the *saltu* they could get at.

He laughed and assured her he'd found variety was the spice of life. The old saw translated into Spanish as a new and clever one she'd never heard before. So she laughed like hell and said as long as he liked variety there were some really wicked tricks she'd been wanting to try for some time, if ever she found a real sport who wouldn't accuse of her of being *loco en la cabeza* just for trying it between *las chupas* or up *el roto*.

So in the end Longarm was glad they'd brought along plenty of water. For he sure had to wash a lot of her off his privates with naptha soap and a string rag once he'd had her every way a man could have a woman, along with a couple he was sure she'd just invented.

Chapter 7

Once it got light enough the next morning, Longarm explored out to their west on foot while the gals brewed some of his genuine Arbuckle coffee over a bitty Indian fire well inside the walls.

He soon found, as he'd hoped, a serious wagon trace running almost due west from the old trail stop. The winds and rains of many a year had tried to heal the desert pavement where countless wheels and even more hooves had busted through the caliche to form a new firm surface almost a yard down. It reminded him of the notorious Bloody Lane back at Antietam, save for not being filled from one high bank to the other with bloody, shattered bodies.

Nobody had planned the Bloody Lane ahead of that bloodiest day of the war. Like this one, a mess of hooves and wagon wheels, in that case bound for a gristmill on Antietam Creek, had worn the original grade down to where it wouldn't wear any deeper. He stamped the hard, dusty surface experimentally. It felt like macadamized pavement underfoot. That was doubtless why he couldn't decide whether some of those windblown dusty crescents were hoof marks or not. He figured at least some of them had to be when, another few furlongs west, he came upon a windrow of horse apples, fresh enough for flies and tumble bugs to be working on.

He stared soberly off as far to the west as he could see. He saw nothing but waist-high stickerbrush and, here and there, a saguaro standing taller, like a holdup victim reaching for the sky with its thorny gray-green arms.

The western sky behind them was a shade of dusty rose. It shouldn't have been at this time of the day on the Sonora Desert. The sun was already shining warm on Longarm's back from the east. He wet a finger with his lips and held it up to test such breeze as there might be. The dry desert air was moving slow and sneaky from the west. He doubted it would be all that dry ere long. He turned and retraced his steps to the tree-shaded ruins, muttering, "Red sky in the morning, Sailor take warning."

He didn't feel all that much like a sailor, but the same rule of thumb applied on the desert as well as the sea. Despite the cloudless cobalt blue overhead and the white hot dazzle to the east, the sky to the west was red because the sunlight was lancing almost horizontal into wetter air, a heap of wetter air, coming their way with the slow but steady west wind.

As he rejoined Moreno and the two Pima gals around the bitty breakfast fire, he announced, "It's going to rain fire and salt by siesta time and we'll be a lot drier outside these mud walls. Our *feet* will, at least, and we don't want any bedding or supplies on the dirt once it's one big puddle, either."

Moreno rose to his feet, stared soberly to the west through a gap in the walls and said, "We got time for to drink plenty of coffee, at least. I have been out in this sort of country during a rainstorm. It would be impossible to sleep if there was anywhere dry for to lie down. Do you know why there is always so much lightning when it rains on cactus?"

Longarm hunkered down by the fire and helped himself to a tin can of black coffee as he decided, "Reckon it takes a stronger than usual rainstorm to do the job. If it was easy to rain in desert country, there wouldn't be any deserts."

Coffee alone wouldn't do it, so once he'd downed two cups he opened one of his last cans of beans. He was getting mighty tired of beans. But since they were running out of them, thanks to all this unexpected company, things evened out.

The gals wanted to go back to bed before it got really hot and sweaty. They didn't say with whom. Longarm glanced up through the overhead branches before he pointed out, "It's liable to rain before it shines enough to worry about. I wish someone would pay attention to a man when he wasn't just making sweet talk. It's time to load up and move out, while we can pack things dry. I just hate the way wet bedding smells when you unroll it after a long sticky ride."

Moreno backed him. The gals quit pouting when, just about the time they had the stock saddled with most everything they'd be taking along packed, big globs of warm rain commenced to land all about in the dust as if the overhead buzzards were acting sassy.

Chiflada wailed in her own lingo. Rita wailed in Spanish that even if they didn't drown their palm fruit was certain to spoil.

Longarm had a better idea. They loaded the two heavily laden baskets on either side of an empty saddle and lashed a tarp over both. That allowed Longarm to shelter his now unprotected bedroll and one gal, along with himself, under the good old army poncho he'd been smart enough to bring along instead of his usual slicker.

It was just as well the adventurous Pima gals had decided they wanted to swap partners again. Rita was skinnier as well as prettier. There was barely room for a man big as Longarm and a gal small as Rita under that finite amount of rubberized canvas and, since there was only one hole in the middle for both their heads to stick up through, it might have got more tedious rubbing faces on the trail with the sort of pumpkin-headed Chiflada.

They wound up sort of rubbing faces because Rita decided the best way to fit both their behinds in the same saddle was for her to ride backwards, her tailbone braced against the swells of his McClellan and her thighs spread over his as he balanced for them both with his feet in the stirrups.

By the time they had all this worked out, it was raining more serious and they were a couple of furlongs west on El Camino Diablo, if that was really it. She squirmed to get more comfortable, for her, as she held on with her arms around his waist under the poncho and murmured, red-faced as Indians could get, "About the naughty way I behaved last night, *querido* . . ."

"I generally wear this ankle-length oil cloth slicker," he cut in, not recalling the Spanish for slicker. She looked even more confused than she should have for just one foreign word, so he explained, "If I had that one the two of us wouldn't fit under it. Not this dry, in any case. Fortunately I remembered how uncomfortable form-fitting waterproofing can feel in warm weather and decided on this army poncho instead. It doesn't stand out at such a distance as my best slicker, should there be any Yaqui this far west. I've bought a bunch of slickers in all styles and colors since the first time I was caught by a real western gullywasher. This yellow one, made in New England for the fishing trade, keeps me dry enough, but I always worry about being spotted from the next state. You see, they make them bright yellow so that should a fisherman be swept overboard in a howling gale . . ."

"*Querido,* I am trying to tell you how sorry I am," she cut in, adding, "I do not know what could have come over me last night. I was angry with you, a little, for turning away from me to stand watch when I was feeling so passionate, and then when my cousin suggested we do . . . what we did . . ."

Longarm kissed her, it was easy, and soothed, "If you *muchachas* hadn't been as naturally curious as the rest of us, I might have gone to my grave wondering if I'd missed anything."

She laughed, kissed him harder, and reached down between them to work on his fly as she said, "*Ay, Maria, Madre de Dios,* life is so short, death is so long, and even while we live we get so few chances for to have a little innocent fun."

It seemed a mite late to ask, but as long as he still had the chance he gulped and said, "I, ah, washed myself with soap and water by the dawn's early light. I know for a fact that your cousin did, too."

As she got her small hand inside his pants to see how big she could make him she soothed, "*Ay, que linda,* I can feel how fresh and clean your soft flesh is. *Pero* for why is it still soft? Do you take me for a *chochina mentho* who would go through the day without cleaning her *cosita* after a night of romantic amusement?"

He felt somewhat reassured but it might not have made all that much difference to him or any other man with feelings once she had his *pitón* and *cojones* out of his fly, hanging on as if she thought she was gripping a saddlehorn for Pete's sake.

He was walking their damned mount as it plodded ever onward in the warm downpour, head down and tail dripping. Longarm only needed one hand on the reins, under their mutual poncho, and she had a good grip on his waist as well as his poor dong, so he went exploring with his free hand to find her yellow skirts up around her bare rump with naturally nothing under it as she tried to slide closer on the split leather at an interesting angle, one thigh hooked over the grips of his cross-draw sixgun like so.

It was impossible to get it all the way in, that way. When she said it was deep enough to suit her, anyhow, he told her to speak for herself. But he had to be a good sport, teasing as it felt, or just dismount and rut in the mud with her like a love-struck hog.

For the sunken road they were following was fetlock deep in muddy rainwater, now, with a noticeable current to the west as well, when a man took time to study on it.

He didn't have much time to study on anything as they rode that way, letting the movements of the saddle under them do most of the work because of how hard it was to hump serious in such a delightfully awkward position. Rita was trying to keep most of her hair dry under the broad brim of his Stetson by kissing him wetly all over his face as she gasped, *"Ay, que atormento dulce!* I know I would climax right away if only I could move freely, *pero* this is beautiful as well because I have never been right on the edge this way for half so long!"

He chuckled fondly and said, "It sure helps pass the time on a rainy day. But while we're having all this fun we'd still better keep our guard up."

She purred, "I love what you have up me, *querido mio!"*

He said, "My pleasure, señorita. I meant others who might not feel as friendly toward you or me right now. Everything ahead and out to either side fades to foggy gray less than a *vara* off in this rain. But I can probably spot anyone laying for us close to the trail out ahead of us. How do things look behind us, as long as you're in such a good position to know?"

She craned to stare back over his shoulder as she bit down on the third of his shaft inside her with her internal contractions and laughed sort of dirty. She tongued his ear and said, "My cousin and your prisoner are having fun back there, too. *Pero* from the way he has her head down over their mount's mane I would say she is being more wicked than I. The old ones say *muchachas* who let a lover *pela las nalgas* too often can catch all sorts of fevers. *Pero* some women seem to like it better that way."

"You don't say," replied Longarm, innocently as he rose in the stirrups to get deeper in this ridiculous but doubtless more sanitary position as he added, "Never mind what they're doing behind us. Keep an eye out for anyone following us further back. I know at least one rider has to be out ahead of us. Yaqui or *rurales* good as me at reading sign could be after him, them, or *us*. Moreno and me left more than one horse apple getting this far, and of course anyone who knows this country at all would know about this old road we're on, whether it's the one we were looking for or not."

She didn't answer. He didn't care, until they'd both finished coming, thanks to that new angle and extra inch he had up inside her. As she felt him ejaculating in her she sobbed,

"Don't take it out! Don't ever take it out, *querido!*"

So he didn't. It felt grand, if somewhat less frantic, to just ride on through the rain, letting it soak up inside her as their mutual swaying in the saddle kept it up for them both with no effort on their part.

They came three times that way, over a period of almost that many hours. Then the rain let up, the sun came back out, and it was soon too hot under the poncho for them. So they took it off, he buttoned up decent, and he dismounted to let her ride more demure as he led afoot, easing his poor stiff hips by walking the kinks out.

The walking wasn't as easy as it had been, further east before the unexpected rain. The grade of the sunken road was steeper and the winding ruts gouged by running water were way deeper. So a man or beast had to pay more attention to where he planted a foot or a hoof.

It hadn't rained that long or that hard. He knew he and all four ponies were playing hopscotch over the results of many a long ago gully washer and likely some wind storms as well. The light rain they'd just had had only served to wash away any recent sign ahead. Longarm would have bet nobody had been down this way ahead of them in years, had not he found those fresh horse apples, earlier.

He started watching farther ahead and all around for some shade, knowing how much they might need some as the sun rose ever higher in the clearing sky. He spied no likely shade, but, on the other hand, the heat seemed to be holding back, mayhaps because there was so much wet caliche to dry out before it could get back to baking the air above it, or mayhaps because the sky wasn't all that clear by desert standards. Aside from scattered clouds sweeping the surrounding desert with dark patches of shade, the sun itself seemed to be shining down through cobwebs. So there had to be a lot of shit still up there betwixt the galloping clouds.

As if to prove his point, a bolt from the blue, or dry lightning, the most dangerous kind, split a tall saguaro less than a quarter mile south with a bodacious thunderclap, spooking humankind and horseflesh alike.

That was one of the things that made dry lightning so dangerous. A man or even a beast could get braced for lightning strikes in the midst of a good storm with plenty of wind and rain to warn one. The sudden sizzle and bang out of what had seemed a friendly sky upset hell out of all four ponies. Longarm hung onto the ones packing his McClellen, old Rita, and their palm fruit. Back up the sunken road, Moreno managed the pony he and Chiflada had been humping on. But the lighter-laden bay he'd been leading busted loose to go tearing back the way they'd just come, trailing two thirds of its lead line. Moreno waved the third left at Longarm, wailing, "Was not my fault, the *chingado* rawhide must have been weakened by all that rain!"

Longarm considered replacing Rita in his own saddle to chase after the runaway. It had already run quite a ways and if it didn't break one of its own fool legs tearing that sudden over cut-up roadway, nobody with a lick of sense was going to follow it that suicidal. So he yelled, "Let it go. It'll likely get lonesome for the rest of our stock once it gets over its spook. If it don't, we can manage without such a *caballo loco*."

Moreno called back he hadn't even considered chasing the runaway, adding, "I am under arrest and you got all the guns, no?"

Longarm said that was about the size of it and they moved on. The heat held off past noon. Longarm took advantage of the break in the usual August weather to take as much time as possible while the desert didn't seem to care. El Camino Diablo was behaving more like a dry wash than an old wagon trace by now. Earlier rains as well as that recent one had washed all sorts of thorny driftwood down into it from the higher ground all about. But the tricky footing didn't worry Longarm as much as the limited view as he found the banks to either side rising shoulder high or more.

He led the way topside, remounted with Rita riding in a more refined position behind him, clinging to his waist with her rump on his bedroll, and followed El Camino Diablo, he hoped, from out a ways to the north. There was nothing he could do about the dotted lines of hoofprints they were punching through the caliche between the clumps of brush and cactus as they wound ever on to the west. Riders who didn't want to leave a clear trail across open desert just had no business riding across open desert. He could only hope nobody trying to cut their trail would be trying this far from where they'd last ridden across such firm crust.

The sun was shining in their faces, albeit not as ferociously as usual for a desert afternoon, when they came upon what seemed a highway planned for and laid-out by mice, or maybe rabbits, tops.

Rita still said, with a wistful sigh, it was the game trail she and her cousin could follow home. So that was where they got off, with their heavy baskets. All four of them agreed it was too bad it had gotten so late in the day. The Pima gals said they'd barely make it home for supper if they started from there right now, running.

Pima ran good, albeit neither gal was running fast enough to catch a rabbit as they lit out to the south with their big fruit baskets bobbing like cottontail rumps.

Neither looked back. Longarm wondered why he was staring after 'em so long and turned to his prisoner, growling, "*Vamanos, pendejo romántico,* before they tell their brothers about your mistreatment of that fat one's *culo.*"

Moreno laughed and asked if perchance he heard an *olla* calling a *caldera* black as they rode on in restored humor.

They'd ridden no more than an hour when, resting the ponies atop a gentle rise, Moreno commented on the mirage ahead. Longarm nodded at what seemed a fair-sized shimmersome lake a mile or less down El Camino Diablo and agreed it sure looked real. He added, "I know the spirit lakes of the Great Basin and Mojave better, but I have seen 'em with the low afternoon sun blazing off the imaginary water like that. That one's a real pisser, considering what a cool day we've had out here, so far. You see 'em more often late in the day after some serious sunbaking."

Moreno scowled at the astoundingly real-looking lake ahead and decided, *"Pues . . . no se . . .* I have seen my share of such illusions and that one even *smells* like stagnant mudflats, no?"

Longarm sniffed the warm gentle breezes from the west, blinked, and decided, "Aw, shit, you've got *me* imagining things with my own nose, you superstitious Mex. Let's ride on and you'll see that mirage recede into the sunset ahead of us."

They never. It only took them eight or ten minutes, at a trot, to reach the real muddy shore of one mighty impressive playa, or occasional desert lake. The old wagon trace they'd been following ran directly down into its likely shallow depths to emerge Lord-only-knew-where. Squinting into the low sun Longarm could see why all that rainwater had wound up impounded here. The far shore was higher and covered with folds of what looked from his side like road tar. He told Moreno, "Lava flat. Likely left over from before your Aztec ancestors were so mean to Cortez. I doubt even a Mex teamster would want to drive over razor-sharp glassy bubbles. So it's a safe bet the road winds some, out yonder under all that muddy water."

Longarm stood in his stirrups to gaze north and south. The mirrorlike playa stretched far as he could see either way, meaning at least six or eight miles. As he settled back in his saddle, he decided, "It's a toss-up either way, but going around the north end takes us closer to the border and hence border-patrolling sons of bitches in big sombreros. So I vote we circle around the south end."

Moreno asked if he got to vote. Longarm laughed, not unkindly, and said, "Not hardly. We both know you wouldn't be headed *anywhere* with me if you had any *say* in the matter."

Chapter 8

The sun was about down but bouncing more gloaming than usual off the unseasonable clouds above them by the time they'd worked around the south end of the ten-or twelve-mile playa. A tall saguaro standing in the shallows with its arms held up for mercy had split its green thorny hide from its soaking roots up. It would likely die once the playa receded and all the rainwater stored in its swollen pulp leaked out as the air went oven-dry again.

They followed the western shore no more than a furlong before they saw what looked like elephant hide pillows piled between the stickerbrush and cactus to their left. It was a lava flat, all right, and a big one. It was odd how sometimes you could see where lava had run down off some prehistoric volcano out this way while other times, such as this, the lava had just spread out like blackstrap molasses that had bubbled up from hell on its own. The high country of Mexico was all broken out in volcanic cones and plugs. But the Sonora Desert was notorious for its big flat scabs of unrecorded injuries to the earth's crust. As they tried to work up the shore betwixt the cooled lava and tepid water, it got easier to see why so much runoff had been strapped there. The general slope was to the west. The lava had boiled up through a north-south crack, a big one, to dam the natural drainage in these parts as it turned to solid rock.

They came to a tongue of lava that ran right out into the playa, blocking further easy riding along the sandy shoreline with its six or eight feet jumble of glassy basalt, smooth or jagged as the lava had contracted on cooling, likely centuries ago. It looked brand new. Basalt was like that where it didn't get rained on a lot.

The light was getting as tricky as the footing ahead. So Longarm reined in and said, "We may as well camp here for now and push on after moonrise. There's driftwood all about for the last of our coffee. We'll have time to catch a couple of winks apiece before the moon's high enough and the coffee's got us going again."

As they dismounted, Moreno gathered all the reins to lead the three ponies to water, unbidden. He was learning how to get along with his fair but firm captor. Longarm moseyed back to that dead, decayed, and fallen saguaro they'd just passed and proceeded to stomp it to kindling with his boot.

Saguaro, growing somewhat confused as to whether it was a cactus or a tree, had a spongy skeleton of real wood imbedded in its soft green pulp. The big, slow-growing cacti lived long as a lot of trees, as well, but once they died, as all things living must, their woody skeletons came in handy. Aside from kindling and light structural members for temporary shacks, the Mex folk used slabs of the lacy gray saguaro wood as window screening, lantern covers, and such.

Longarm just wanted to brew some damned coffee. So he busted up enough for the kindling he'd need to get some dead greasewood going. By the time he was hunkered near the wall of lava to put a match to the tidy, careful pile, his prisoner had watered, unsaddled, and rubbed down the three ponies. Longarm was glad he hadn't had to tell a *vaquero* gone wrong how important that might be, now that they'd lost one of their spare mounts in such shitty surroundings.

By the time they'd consumed the coffee and some ironwood nuts Longarm had gathered back at those ruins, it was fair dark. Knowing it would stay that way for a spell, Longarm marched Moreno back along the shore to where a clump of smoke-tree had sprouted from a crack in the shoulder-high wall of lava. As he cuffed Moreno to a branch, the prisoner complained, *"Ay, mierda,* do we have to go through this every night?"

To which Longarm could only reply, "Not when I can keep my damned eyes open and not at all once I get you to Denver, old son."

He unclipped his derringer, replaced the two live rounds with the blanks he'd improvised, and handed it to the prisoner, saying, "You know how it goes 'til I come back for you. If I ain't back by moonrise feel free to fire once and wake me up. If you fire twice I'll know it's more important."

Moreno sat down, sulky, with the derringer in his free fist and his back to the lava wall in the inky shadows of the smoke-tree. So Longarm had a last look around and said, *"Bueno.* I doubt anything more dangersome than a lizard will come our way over all that jagged-ass lava to our north or west. Nobody with a lick of sense would ride out of the east across the uncertain bottom of that spooky playa. So you only have to stay awake and keep one eye on the trail we just left to the south."

"Gracias. Have you forgotten *you* had both those Indias, too?" asked Moreno, morosely.

Longarm chuckled and said, "That's why I'm giving their brothers first crack at *you.* I'll let you catch a few winks before we ride on. So try to stay awake 'til I relieve you, hear?"

Moreno told him to do something to himself that sounded downright painful. Longarm ambled back to the dying fire, made sure the three ponies were tethered where they could get at both the water and some *petota,* a sort of sorry-looking but edible weed related to what they called miner's lettuce up in the Motherlode Country.

Even a dying fire could be seen mighty far on a moonless night on the desert. So he kicked theirs out. Then he made sure all their canteens were not only filled but wet on their woolly outsides to cool good as that water evaporated. Then, having tended all the chores he might overlook, waking up full of black coffee, he spread his bedding on the sand and turned in for forty winks, removing his hat, vest, and gunbelt but leaving the rest of his duds on. It got cold on the desert at night when a gent was forced to sleep alone.

He was asleep in no time, after all that action the night before and an all-day ride. He naturally didn't recall falling asleep, one never did, but he knew he'd just been asleep when his eyes popped open to regard the rising moon as his ears were still working on what they'd just heard. He started to reach for the sixgun he'd left safe from drifting sand in his nearby inverted hat. A sinister male voice told him not to move a *chingado* muscle if he wanted to go on living, so he didn't, as he cursed Moreno's ancestry all the way back to Adam and Eve.

There were three *rurales,* he saw, looming between him and the only way out of this dead end in the moonlight. The moon wasn't all that bright, but hardly anyone else wore those tall, peaked sombreros and bolero jackets with *buscadero* gunbelts and crossed bandoliers. He knew he'd guessed right when one of the *rurales* said, "Listen to me very careful, Brazo Largo."

"Who's Brazo Largo?" tried Longarm, as that translated to English.

The *rurale* snapped, *"Silencío!* I am speaking. You are listening, if you wish for to be taken in alive. We know your reputation for sleight-of-hand with weaponry. You will now put both hands up, as far as they can reach, and then you will very slowly follow them up in a most predictable manner. If you take too deep a breath or have a bit of trouble with your balance I shall fire and at the moment this gun in my hand is trained upon your *cajones,* you *pendejo gringo!"*

Longarm sighed, raised his hands, and sat up, his mind awhirl as he tried to clear the last cobwebs from it. For this was a serious son-of-a-bitching situation, thanks to that son-of-a-bitching Moreno.

He didn't think this was the time to ask them if they'd already killed Moreno. There was an outside chance they'd missed him, riding right past his smoke-tree cover and

Moreno did have that derringer but, shit, how many *rurales* could anyone shoot with blanks?

The one holding that gun on him purred, "That's right, big gringo gunman, roll to one knee, and now rise, *pero muy lento,* eh?"

Longarm was willing, unwilling as he was to go along with them, but then somebody else yelled, "Brazo Largo, *esquivar!*" which meant "Duck!" so he dove for the dirt as a .45 slug bored through the space he'd just been in while that particular *rurale* screamed like a goosed virgin with Moreno's thrown pig sticker stuck in his porcine back!

Then Moreno had dropped the other two with well-placed rounds of .44-40 as they'd whirled toward the sound of his voice, too late. By the time all three lay sprawled between him and Moreno, two in the dust and one in the shallows of the nearby playa, Longarm had his sixgun in hand, ready for further trouble. But there didn't seem to be any as he caught up with Moreno, by their ponies. Longarm said, "Good thinking," as he helped the young Mex steady the spooked stock. When he saw all three were secure, he added, "Nice shooting, too. I saw them riding past you in this tricksome light and it was my own fault you had that knife. But how in thunder did you drop them last two with them blanks?"

Moreno handed him the derringer, modestly, as he confessed, "I am not the Juan Moreno who robbed that train. *Pero* I *am,* if I may say so, an accomplished *ladrón.*"

Longarm laughed like hell and said, "You helped yourself to some live rounds from my saddlebags whilst I thought both of us were getting laid. It's my own damned fault for neglecting to keep you cuffed every damned minute I didn't have my eye on you!"

"Are you going to punish me, now?" asked the prisoner, only half in jest. For anyone could see Longarm looked mighty chagrined.

The big lawman laughed sheepishly and replied, "Not hardly. You just saved my fool neck. I'm just sore at myself for letting my damn guard down. Come on, let's make sure

I don't get back-shot by a dead *rurale,* you sneaky cuss."

The moon was higher. Longarm still rekindled their fire and lit things up for a serious look-see. The old boys who'd obviously backtracked that runaway pony wearing a *rurale* saddle were dead as they'd ever be. Moreno recovered his knife, wiped it clean with sand and a *rurale* shirttail, and put it away before helping himself to that one victim's gun rig as well as his wallet.

The casual move wasn't lost on Longarm, who glanced up from the one he was examining near the edge of the water to mutter, "Don't go getting silly on me now, old son."

Moreno got to his feet, the sixgun the *rurale* had dropped back in its holster on his own slim hip, as he calmly observed, *"Mierda,* I could have killed you before I killed them if that had been my intention."

Longarm nodded thoughtfully at the prisoner's bare wrists as he decided, "Any professional thief can pick a handcuff lock, given a lot of time on his hands and plenty of privacy. So, *bueno,* you made a fool out of me as well as them, old son. Now I'm asking you polite but for the last time to unbuckle that gun rig, let it fall, and step away from it."

There wasn't quite enough light to see what kind of wheels might be going around in the young owlhoot rider's dark eyes. They stood facing one another at gunfighting range, each man's gun in its holster, for a time some might have described as tense. Then Moreno softly said, "I am pretty good and they tell me it takes a split second longer to cross-draw."

Longarm nodded soberly and said, "You might have an edge, if you'd like to try, Moreno."

The young Mex laughed boyishly and said, "I did not know what you meant the first time you said a few extra days and nights could be most precious to a man no matter what might lie ahead. I do not wish for to die this side of Denver. Just so you know I *could* have killed you instead of them, before they got here, eh?"

Longarm waited until Moreno had disarmed himself before he quietly asked, "Why didn't you, then? It ain't as if I'm taking you in to face charges of indecent exposure, you know."

Moreno nodded and said, "I know. But I am not the Juan Moreno they sent you to bring back. So it has occurred to me that should I get away, they will just keep sending you and others like you after me, no?"

Longarm nodded and said, "That's about the size of it. On the other hand, no matter what you may have heard about our U. S. federal courts, they're more likely to apologize than hang you if and when they find out you're another cuss entire."

Moreno said, "I hope you are right. I have heard bad things about gringo judges and *pobrecitos* such as I. *Pero* you have convinced me at least *some* gringo lawmen are fair-minded."

"It ain't for me to say," warned Longarm.

The kid said, "*Comprendo.* Your job is finished once you turn me over to that judge and if that judge fucks his mother I am done for. *Pero* you told me I would get a fair trial and I think I would rather trust your word than try for to beat you to the draw. So how soon do we ride on from this *chingado* place?"

Longarm smiled wryly and said, "I can see why you might not feel sleepy. First we'll see what else we can salvage off our newfound friends, here. They must have their own ponies back along the shore a ways and let's hope they were packing plenty of coffee, grub, and, please, Lord, some *tobacco.*"

Moreno said they'd ridden past him and tethered their own three ponies just around the bend. So Longarm said, "*Bueno.* Let's get cracking, then. You may as well put that gun back on, for now."

"Do you mean that?" asked his prisoner, warily.

Longarm said, "I wouldn't have said it if I hadn't. There's two of us and Lord knows how many meaner bastards standing betwixt us and Denver, so, 'long as you're ready to come willing, we may as well work together. It has to have *dying* together beat all hollow."

Chapter 9

Los rurales lived well, as their reward for killing folk, so their saddlebags were treasure troves that made Longarm and his armed and dangerous prisoner forgive them for cutting their trail. One of the late *rurales* had smoked expensive but rank cigars that the notoriously pungent Marshal Vail up in Denver might have gagged on. The one Moreno had downed with that skillfully thrown blade had favored sweeter burning *claro* cigars whilst the last had died well-supplied with Negrita Brand cheroots, which were close enough.

The American lawman and his prisoner salvaged more waterproof matches they could use along with coffee from Vera Cruz, ground with more chickory than Longarm preferred, but what the hell.

Their trail grub was U.S. Army Field Rations. El Presidente admired all things gringo but the U.S. Constitution. The U.S. Quartermaster Corps admired Boston Beans and British Bully Beef along with tasteless but filling hardtack biscuits. Those *rurales* had obviously agreed with Longarm and other old soldiers on hardtack. So whilst they'd brought plenty along to feed their ponies, they'd stocked up on tortillas wrapped in corn husks and waxed paper, bless their otherwise useless souls.

The three extra ponies might have come from the same litter as the three Longarm and Moreno already had, save for one who'd thrown a shoe but hadn't started limping yet.

Longarm knew it would once it had been led worth mention over solid lava. So he rid it of its saddle and bridle to fend for itself on the friendly side of the lava flat, where there was a little browse and plenty of water, for as long as a temporary lake might last.

When Moreno asked what a pony running wild was supposed to do once the playa dried up again, entire, Longarm said, "Nothing lasts forever. Meanwhile that much water ought to last more than one generation of fairy shrimp or, hell, even to the next good rain for all we know for certain. Would you rather I just shoot the critter here and now?"

Moreno hesitated, then said, "There was a time I would have said so. Since I have been wondering just how many little bits of forever I have left to enjoy, I am not so certain. Is true one hour of life is worth a billion years of death, and *quien sabe* how many flowers this doomed *caballo* might smell before everything dries out again?"

Longarm said he'd noticed how philosophical old boys tended to get once they found themselves in the shadow of the gallows. He meant it when he told Moreno he hoped some other Juan Moreno had stopped that mail train and gunned that postal worker. They then cut all the philosophy and headed west across the lava in the moonlight.

They led the string of ponies afoot, slow, of course. The moon was bright and a lot of the basaltic rock was shiny. It still could have taken as much as fifty years off a man's life to ride over all that treacherous shit in any light. It wouldn't have done his mount a lick of good, either, when they busted through a lava tube and fell on the razor-sharp results.

Walking low and slow they were able to pick their way where the surface looked most like dead elephants or even someone's neglected backyard. There were considerable patches where wind-blown dust had filled in hollows. Desert weeds and even some grass had sprouted where the shallow rock bowls under their roots held water longer. Longarm had read somewhere how basalt weathered to mighty rich soil, one it weathered at all, say under a few inches of moist muck. That was how come poor folk in lands like Mexico lived right on the slopes of volcanos. They weren't trying to commit suicide. They were trying to raise enough to get by. All five ponies seemed to like the grazing in those lava flat hollows. Longarm let 'em, within reason, since they had to rest 'em at least once an hour, and it would have been needlessly cruel to put 'em on a diet at the same time.

Moreno said he'd noticed from the first how kind Longarm was to stock and other critters. He said, "My people feel women and other lesser beings must be controlled with a firm hand, for to show them who is boss."

Longarm, smoking a Negrita, muttered, "I've been to your chicken fights and watched a torero get all gussied up in fancy duds before he butchers a cow, Spanish style. I thought we'd settled it in that war we had with you-all that we ain't sissies just because we can ride a roan or a redhead without whipping the tar out of neither. Some say our style of roping is crueler than your'n and we do eat way more meat, so I reckon it all evens out. Watch how you jerk the bit of that one you're leading directsome. These Spanish bits your *rurales* use would be against the law if *I* had any say in the matter."

The *vaquero* gone wrong protested, "Hey, it takes a Spanish bit for to control any *caballo* broken in the Spanish style."

Longarm grunted, "That's what I just said. I ain't no sissy who weeps over a cavalry mount reduced to hauling ice. I'd rather haul ice when I got old than wind up in a glue pot, any day. You Mex hands would see some controlling if ever you hired on at the Hash Knife or the Jingle Bob at roundup time. Each and every Anglo hand gets his own string of six or eight ponies to control the shit out of, using up more than one a day during roundup, and he gets fired if the boss wrangler sees he's abused even one of 'em, needless."

Moreno sniffed and said, "You people are rich. You can afford for to pamper your stock, and we all know how you spoil your women."

Longarm swore, started to dispute some more, and gave it up as an exercise in futility. He said, "Let's just say we do things a might different and don't jerk that fucking bit no more, because I've told you not to. Like I told this sweet little Mormon gal one time, I drink coffee because I want to drink coffee and I'm bigger than you. She didn't want me to smoke, neither. Mormon gals can sure get picky about a man's habits, considering how casual they can be about sharing him with half a dozen others."

Moreno brightened and said, "We have some of those in my country. That *ladrón,* El Presidente, sold land to some Mormons who moved down this way when your government told them they could only marry one *mujer* at a time. I understand they are some sort of Protestants, so of course they are all going to hell in the end, no?"

Longarm smiled thinly and replied, "There's some difference of opinion as to who might or might not have the right answer. The point I was trying to make was that I've found it best to do things my way until or unless I meet someone who can make me do things his or her way. So we're going to treat them *caballos* my way and if I'm wrong I'm the one who figures to suffer, right?"

Moreno said, "No. *I* get to suffer, too, if *los rurales* take us both before I let you take me back to Denver."

Longarm cocked a brow, blew smoke out his nostrils, and decided to let that pass. The kid had had his chance to bust loose, dirty, and it seemed smarter to lead him on gentle than jerk his bit by reminding him, needlessly, just who was in command of this infernal expedition.

It took them until almost dawn to work their way across all that treacherous lava without hurting either themselves or the ponies. As soon as they found themselves back aboard good old crunchy caliche, Longarm said, "*Bueno,* let's scout for some shade. There ought to be mesquite close to the edge of the rocks. We don't want to go much further without finding where El Camino Diablo runs on to the west."

Moreno was smart enough to see why they wanted to follow a road across such uncertain country. But he'd assumed the old wagon trace simply ran across the bottom of that flooded playa, straight across if not under the lava, and from there on west, more or less along the same east-west line.

Mounting up to rest his ass as they walked their ponies north along the west front of the lava flow, Longarm explained to Moreno, as the latter got back in his own saddle, "The old-timey teamsters found the easy way, not the shortest way, after no doubt a heap of trial and error. This froze-up lava was here long before any wagon trace. So the road can't go under it and it could hardly go over it, judging from how bumpsome we just found it with no *wheels* to worry about."

"How then?" Moreno demanded.

Longarm pointed north with his chin and said, "Around one end or the other, of course. We just proved it wasn't the south end. That leaves the north. The reason I want to search for the detour by day is in hopes of saving us some serious detouring. I'd hate to ride for hours only to find by the dawn's early light we'd rid right across the damned route and had to backtrack."

Moreno thought and decided, "*Comprendo*. Would make no sense for to circle the far end and cling to the lava all the way south to where one was free for to move on to the west."

Longarm replied, "That's what I just said. I figure we might be able to navigate by the sun at a forty-five degree angle to the northwest, which ought to cross El Camino Diablo sooner or later no matter where in thunder they run it around the north end of this infernal lava flat."

They rode on in thoughtful silence for a time as the sky to the east began to purl gray. Longarm pointed with his chin again to call back, "I see a tolerable grove of mesquite ahead. Likely where water run before that lava dammed the drainage. Mesquite can't grow where there's none at all, but they sure can sink their roots if they've a mind to."

Moreno said, "I see them. I see we are in for a hot, dry day as well. So tell me, what if the old ones did not simply cut around the north end of this lava? What if El Camino

Diablo runs on to the north toward some other easy passage, water hole, or whatever, before it winds on to the sea?"

Longarm took a last wistful drag on his Negrita and grumbled, "I sure wish you wouldn't ask such intelligent questions, you fool Mex."

Chapter 10

Men around a campfire tend to brag on wonders they've done, seen, eaten, or screwed. Longarm didn't like to brag, preferred his grub plainer than his women, and didn't think much of kissing and telling, so Moreno got to do most of the talking that evening and by the time Longarm said it was getting late and that he'd stand the first watch he was better than half convinced they'd sent him to pick up the wrong Juan Moreno.

He'd asked trick questions as the young Mex had bragged. When that hadn't worked he bragged just enough himself to raise at least one eyebrow on anyone who'd ever ridden through Colorado or, hell, the northern halves of Texas or New Mexico Territory.

But Moreno hadn't blinked when Longarm had located Denver on the Arkansas and run the South Platte across the Staked Plains of Texas. He seemed willing to accept saguaro cactus and mesquite up around Loveland and never blinked when told about the swell church picnics held in Denver's Estes Park.

Estes Park, of course, was that big patch of grazing up around Long's Peak and not a city park at all. But of course he might have been braced for a poker bluff whenever the conversation turned to the parts of this world that mail train had been anywheres near when it was stopped by that mixed gang of Anglo and Mex riders.

Longarm could see how even a trustworthy informer could mix up one Juan Moreno with another. This one bragged on stealing more than one cow, and twice as many women, on both sides of the border. Anyone who talked so big had to be sort of infamous in many a flophouse and back alley dive. Longarm noticed nothing Moreno bragged on added up federal enough for all this fuss. That didn't mean he couldn't be a mighty slick liar, of course.

Meanwhile, they needed each other and Moreno had proven he was slick enough to savvy as much.

Daydreaming dudes like old Hank Thoreau might brag about squatting all alone by Walden Pond, communing with nature, and not needing shit from any other poet. But Longarm had noticed Thoreau's long-suffering pal, Emerson, had been paying the taxes on that particular neck of the woods all the time Thoreau was out there playing hermit. There hadn't been any Indian or bear trouble for quite a spell, either.

Longarm had built their small Indian fire between thick mesquite and a lava back-wall with Yaqui in mind. Reaching for his Winchester with a barely suppressed yawn, he told Moreno, "Try to catch a few winks. I'll take the first watch and wake you when I figure you've had enough. Lord knows when we'll find this grand a spot to bed down again. We got us some daylight riding ahead until we cut El Camino Diablo some more."

"Is going to be hotter than a nun's pillow at a cardinal's convention," Moreno pointed out, pointing up at the low-flying stars as he added, "There is just enough spit in the wind, now, for to make the *chingado* heat sultry instead of dry. Will be a sweatbox by noon if we find shade and who said we shall find any shade, eh?"

Longarm pointed out that was all the more reason for getting a good night's rest while they still had the chance.

So Moreno turned in. Longarm climbed up on some glassy lava with his Winchester and long before midnight he was frozen stiff. Moreno had been right about the moisture in the air. Desert nights were always cool. Wet desert nights were downright clammy. When he finally woke Moreno he told the kid to hang on to a sleep-warmed flannel blanket and throw his poncho on over it. By the time the Mex woke wide enough to see why he was saying dreadful things about Longarm's poor old mother.

Longarm yawned indulgently and replied, "I would piss on your father's grave if even your mother could tell us who he might have been." So the Mex sighed, *"Come mierda y manajate!"* and wandered off to take a leak, plot murder, or whatever.

Considering that made it surprisingly tough to fall asleep in his own roll, weary as Longarm was. He finally did because he had to and in the morning Moreno proved how good he was with a gun, as well as how much he could be trusted with one, for now.

Longarm jumped sideways a full fathom and came down facing the other way with his own .44-40 in hand when Moreno's *rurale* sixgun went off, unexpected, behind him.

Fortunately for the two of them he spotted the still writhing but headless diamondback in the sun-dappled dust between them before he could shoot the fool Mex. So he lowered the muzzle of his own sidearm as he nodded stiffly and said, "*Gracias*. I'm a live-and-let-live gent as a rule, but that was closer to my ass than I generally want eight feet of rattler."

Moreno reloaded as he modestly observed, *"De nada,* that is for why I shot it. It must have been denned somewhere in that lava wall and between us and the morning sun it was acting confused. Big for this sort of country, no?"

Longarm reholstered his own gun, bent over, and picked up the still twitching serpent to whirl it around thrice and send it flying up on the lava as he observed, "Up Arizona way you get ones that size around rocks where there's water enough for rabbit and rats. The bitty sidewinders like their desert sandier and a mite more dry. I'm glad that wasn't a sidewinder. We got enough on our plate without damned sand dunes drifting about to confuse the shit out of us when we don't know where we are to begin with!"

They ate, saddled fresh mounts, and rode out to the northwest while the sun still hung low in the east. It still managed to lash out at them across the chaparral and cactus flats. There was nothing they could do but keep riding, if they ever meant to cut the wagon trace they'd lost under all that flood water the day before.

There was no sign anything bigger than a rabbit had been this way since that last rain. Glancing back, Longarm was hardly cheered by the clear trail they were leaving in the desert pavement. The chalky surface caliche was dry and brittle as ever. The softer soil under it was still damp. Five ponies sure punched a heap of crisp neat holes in their travels. Them transcendental dudes old Hank Thoreau hung out with could have followed a trail clear as that, all the way from Walden Pond, if they'd had a mind to.

He was more worried about less poetic sons of bitches, riding for either side in the ongoing Yaqui uprising. He asked Moreno about any rebel bands he knew of in these parts. Moreno said no rebel with a lick of sense wanted to liberate such disgusting land as part of that land reform they liked to jaw about. He didn't ask Moreno how they figured to divvy Mexico up fair and square among so many hardscrabble peons. He knew Moreno didn't know. Rebel leaders Longarm knew better had explained they had to liberate the land before they could divvy it up. They didn't want to hear a gloomy gringo's simple arithmetic. No doubt the Irish rebels would be able to divide the ten thousand or less square miles of Irish farmland to the satisfaction of no more than a few million farm families, once they got rid of old Queen Victoria. But had he been running either revolution he'd have promised his followers the vote and a bill of rights, not pie in the sky by and by.

He lit another Negrita, noting he was running low on the same but that there were plenty of cigars left. He got rid of the match, this time with care. For there seemed to be more low scrub and, where nothing that impressive grew, more weeds and even some grass.

Moreno noticed it, too. Longarm turned in the saddle to gaze back a ways, saying, "We're still leaving a clear enough trail for your average country boy to follow. But you're right about the grass, even though you're wrong about it sprouting since that rain."

Riding on, he continued, "To begin with grass don't sprout that sudden, from seed. That stubble you're admiring is only a mite green near the roots, meaning it's coming back to life after that rain. But it's been there all the time, straw from the roots up or not. Deserts are like that. This stretch supports more life for some reason. Might be the way the rare rains run off, might be the way the soil retains such rain as may fall, but we're coming on a *llano* either way."

No *vaquero* gone wrong had to ask a gringo what a *llano* was. The literal translation to English would have been a plain or prairie but, just as no Anglo cowhand or Mex *vaquero* meant exactly a table when he said "mesa" or exactly a Christmas tree when he said "piñon," a *llano,* in cow country, was a particular sort of grassy stretch, halfway between desert and prairie. You could graze stock on it, if you were careful. Lots of stockmen did, and weren't. That was how come a heap of southwest range the old timers had recorded as *llano* was pure dusty, these days. Forging on over ever thicker sod, they saw nobody had been grazing this range serious in living memory, if ever. They were soon leaving no trail at all, once the chaparral thinned out to scattered clumps on a tawny carpet of shortgrass.

That was the good part. After that they were even more lost. For when Longarm reined in on a rise to stand in the stirrups and gaze on ahead he saw nothing but more of the same, clean to the uncertain horizon. Leading the way on with a thoughtful frown, he told Moreno, "If I didn't know better I could swear we were lost on the Staked Plains up Texas way. How in blue blazes are we supposed to find a damned wagon trace when anyone can see one way's as good as any other to haul a blamed wagon over all this gently rolling grass!"

Moreno suggested, "Why don't we just swing more to the west and simply keep going until we hit the Sea of Cortez, eh?"

Longarm shook his head and said, "That ain't the way things work, even on the Staked Plains. They call 'em the Staked Plains because all around the edges and up many a canyon the innocent-looking range rises high in the Texas sky on what look like 'dobe stakes or tight-packed pillars. No matter what you call 'em it smarts like hell to ride off such high and sudden cliffs. So it helps to know where you might be heading on the Staked Plains. I don't know *what* in tarnation we could ride off of, into, or whatever if we just beelined blind across all *this* grass. If it was easy to get to from more than a few directions there'd be more stock and less grass around here by now."

He pointed at a shockingly green patch off to their right as he added, "Look at all that salt clover with bumble bees hovering above it! If there was even deer or bighorn in these parts, that salty salad would be gone, not in blossom, this late in the summer!"

Moreno shrugged and said, "Perhaps is too much dry country for to cross between here and other such range, no?"

Longarm nodded but decided, "There's more pressure than that to keep so much grazing dispopulated. Might be bad water, might be bad hunting practices. I know they say noble savages don't kill off all the game the way your kind and mine do. They say that do you put a tooth under your pillow a good fairy will swap you a penny for it, too. Meanwhile, where's that infernal El Camino Diablo?"

"There is something going on, more to our west," Moreno pointed out. Longarm spied the buzzards, too, as the young Mex decided, "I don't know whether they could be over a more traveled route or not. I'll bet you they are over *something*."

Longarm didn't feel like betting against a sure thing. He wasn't sure he wanted to ride that way, either. The old wagon trace they were searching for figured to lie more ahead, unless, of course, it curved south after trending north a ways.

He said, "We'd better have a look-see. If there was nothing over yonder them birds wouldn't be wheeling above it. If it was dead they'd have already spiraled down."

Moreno pointed out, "Unless something is dead and something else won't let them at it."

To which Longarm could only reply, "That's what I meant. Hang back a piece with the ponies and let me take the lead."

"Do not let me stop you," said Moreno, adding, "*Pero* what if you are riding into some sort of ambush?"

Longarm chuckled dryly and said, "Well, shit, you never wanted to come back to Denver with me to begin with, did you?"

Chapter 11

A riderless pony found them before they could find out what was going on. It was a pretty little palomino mare, packing a somewhat oversized center-fire saddle with the wood of its cantle and swells exposed, albeit varnished and waxed.

The mysterious mare spotted them and their own stock about the same time and loped over to join them, nickering with relief as she trailed her reins across the grass by waltzing sort of sideways.

She was way more interested in their mounts than in either of them. So it was Moreno who managed to grab her trailing reins and calm her down with some soothesome cussing. Once he had he swung out of his *rurale* saddle to claim her with his own rump, loudly announcing, "He who touches my *mujer* or my *caballa* dies!"

Longarm smiled thinly and called back, "We'd best find out who was riding her before you. She's packing you a mite docile for a pony prone to buck and bolt."

They rode on. Those high-flying buzzards might have been wheeling a mite closer, now. It was hard to say for certain. A shift in the morning breezes carried the crackle of distant small arms fire. It was hard to judge how distant on rolling range. Longarm lowered his voice as he decided, "A tad to the left of straight ahead. How far is up for grabs. During the war, folk dwelling near or far from battlefields heard the damnedest sounds, or sometimes no sounds at all."

But as they worked their way almost smack under the overhead buzzards there was no mistaking the range and direction of a serious firefight in progress over the next serious rise.

Longarm reined, hauled out his saddle gun, and directed Moreno to stay put with all the ponies. Then he dismounted to leg it the rest of the way to the grassy crest with his Winchester, aiming for a handy clump of what they called soapweed on the northern ranges and yucca down this way.

By either name it was less than knee-high. So he set his hat aside in the dry grass as he crawled the last few yards with his saddle gun to poke his bare head between two bigger blurs of yard-long spines.

Down in the next draw, a dozen two-wheel carts and eight freight wagons, all canvas-covered, were circled tight with the survivors and their stock crowded inside, of course.

Six oxen, four mules, and a couple of ponies lay hither and yon outside the ring, along with four kids, two women, and a man who'd been slower or simply less lucky.

Those who'd made it were blazing away more than they'd have been if Longarm had been in charge down yonder. For the Indians surrounding the party weren't whooping around the wagon circle within easy range. They were afoot, mostly hunkered, better than three hundred yards out. The pissolivers most of the fools down yonder were blazing away with would carry four hundred in still air, but it took shithouse luck to hit anything you were aiming at from seventy-five.

Moreno crept to the crest to join him, whispering, "They're tied to some provident chamisa. My mother warned me curiosity would be the death of me. They're Apache, no?"

Longarm nodded curtly but said, "Kids. What the Lakota call suicide boys and the Nadene, or Apache, call total assholes. They're wearing no medicine paint. That means they're off the reservation with neither their agent's nor their elders' permit. They likely snuck down off the San Carlos or Fort Apache reserve. We're too far west for Mescalero raiders."

Moreno sighed and said, "Is not fair. We got enough of our own *chingado* wild ones in Sonora. For why can't your gringo army keep your own baby-raping Apache on their own side of the border, eh?"

Longarm grimaced and said, "They try, sometimes with more sincerity than skill. Most of the Nadene bands have been behaving, so far, this summer. Like I said, those are kids and you know how kids are. They must have heard about that Yaqui uprising and figured to get in on the fun."

"Como? Yaqui hate Apache as much or more than they hate us!" the young but worldly Mexican observed.

One of the Indians they were discussing jumped to his feet and shook a fistful of trade rifle at the wagon circle.

Longarm said, "They're only encouraging the young rascals. I know how Yaqui and most everyone else feel about Nadene. Apache is a Uto-Aztec term falling somewheres betwixt enemy and motherfucker. But that bunch ain't down here to join forces with the Yaqui. They're out to loot, rape, and ruin whilst they have such a grand opportunity. If I wasn't so smart, them bewildered souls down in yonder wagon circle would doubtless report all this bullshit as a Yaqui attack in the end."

"You mean if any of them lived to report anything," Moreno pointed out, raising his voice a mite to snarl, *"Mierda!* For why are you wasting all your *chingado* ammunition like that, you *pendejos estupidos!"*

Longarm warned, "Keep it down to a roar. We don't even have a covered wagon to duck behind. Let's move back to our ponies. Our best bet is a move against their'n."

As they crawfished back off the crest Moreno frowned thoughtfully and said, "Their what? Their *caballos?* Now that you mention it, they didn't seem to *have* any riding stock!"

Longarm put on his hat and got back to his feet, growling, "They got 'em. Somewheres. Unless you'd like to sell me a reservation jump on foot, from better than a hundred and fifty miles from here."

He explained no further until they'd legged it as far as their own stock, huddled around that clump of chamisa. Moreno had known what he was doing. Chamisa was called "rabbit bush" further north. But rabbits weren't the only critters who liked to browse the rank-smelling yellow flowers.

Longarm wasn't sure why. Rabbit bush smelled like medicine to him and he knew the Indians made a half-ass yellow dye out of them. He hauled his mount's muzzle out of the shrubbery and mounted up as he told Moreno, tersely, what he meant for both of them to try next.

Then he swung his mount around and, Winchester in his free hand, loped it back up the slope to appear upon the skyline, tall in the saddle, to all concerned.

As he'd hoped some might, more than one of the Indians on the slope between him and those wagons reacted to the ominous sight of him by moving to get between him and something he couldn't make out from the crest. Not from the part of the crest he was on at the moment, leastways.

Knowing now which way those spitting and cursing Nadene didn't want him to get to, he heeled his bay hard and loped along the skyline to the south as what seemed the whole Nadene nation proceeded to peg potshots up the slope at him.

Some came frighteningly close. Some had to, despite the range, with so many assholes firing. For assholes, they'd been sort of slick in hiding their own riding stock deeper inside Mexico than your average border raider might have been expected to. As he tore along the crest through a hail of lead he spied the big remuda of Indian ponies bunched in a grassy draw in the care of four smaller tagalongs.

Just then the pony he was riding decided to do a forward somersault. Ponies often did that when they'd taken a rifle ball in their head at full gallop. Longarm landed running and crabbed to one side without slowing as the big brown rump of the already dead pony whipped down to fly-swat anything less agile. As all that horseflesh thudded to the sod behind him, Longarm was already firing from the hip as he continued his charge afoot.

He blew the nearest Nadene kid off his painted pony but held his fire when the little shit sprang back up to run after his mount, bawling to all hundred and four of his guardian spirits. Longarm spared the second one he winged as well, not because they deserved it, but to keep 'em running and bawling after their much nicer ponies. For a basic cavalry tactic, no matter who you might be riding against, was to hit the enemy where it hurt him most, in his riding stock.

Longarm rump-shot a couple of slower ponies to spur the whole remuda on as it lit out in a cloud of dust, bound for the Argentine at least, to hear 'em whinny.

Naturally, the Indians who'd ridden them all the way down from Arizona Territory took exception to Longarm's field tactics and some of them charged his way instead of after their runaway stock.

But that was how come the Winchester Repeating Arms Company of Bridgeport, Connecticut, chambered their .44-40 Model '73 for fifteen rounds. Longarm had half the tube left as he dropped to one knee in the skimpy cover of some more yucca to start aiming serious.

The .44-40 was a compromise between a pistol and a rifle round, designed to let a rider load his saddle gun and side arm from the same handy box. Fired out the longer barrel of a rifle, the forty grains of powder gave the two hundred grains of lead a range of six hundred yards. It took a sharpshooter to come even close at four hundred, and Longarm hated to waste ammo at more than two hundred. So he just paid his puckered asshole no mind and held his fire 'til he knew he'd do better than the three Nadene kids bearing down on him with their own guns blazing away.

When he did fire, aiming well above their bobbing heads to make up for the tricky trajectory, he dropped them just right, gut shot and yelling like coyotes giving birth to busted beer bottles. It wasn't true that Indians didn't yell when they got hurt, unless one gave 'em time to get set for it before you hurt 'em.

That and the rapid pace of their vanishing remuda seemed to discourage those others who were close enough to Longarm to consider him. One stopped a cautious four hundred yards out, waving his own carbine overhead in one hand as he waved his exposed privates at Longarm with the other. To hit a man at that distance called for an elevation almost twice his height. But that old boy sure ran good, once Longarm had fired, for a cusser with one lung blown out.

It was just as well. Longarm's Winchester was empty and he knew better than to let anyone know. He just worked the lever as if to put a fresh round in the chamber as those few Indians who seemed to care just ran on by.

He reloaded as soon as he could, of course. So he was ready for most anything when Moreno called down to him from the crest of the rise. The young Mex had reined in his new palomino near the dead bay Longarm had been riding. As Longarm legged it up the slope he called out, "Where's the rest of the stock? I was out to dismount them, not us!"

Moreno soothed, "Down by the wagons. I did as you told me. I charged from the direction they were not running for to keep them running. By now they must think they were hit by those *chingado rurales*. Is not easy to keep so many *caballos* going the same way at even a lope, on leads. So I dropped them off at the wagons as I followed those *chingado* Apache."

Longarm muttered, "I wish you'd brung at least one along," as he hunkered by the dead pony to examine the damage to his private property. It wasn't bad. Many a stock saddle would have suffered a busted tree from such a hammering. But while General George McClellan had made a piss poor field commander in the war, the rugged army saddle he'd designed was likely the best one ever. Thanks to the solid brass loops provided for lashing on one's possibles, the bodacious crash hadn't even scattered Longarm's bedroll, saddlebags, or canteens. He uncinched the dead carcass and hauled his saddle free, putting his back into it to clear the stirrup and fender on the bottom of the soggy pile. He set that load aside and was hunkered by the poor brute's shot-up head, unbuckling the bridle, when Moreno said, "Here comes the circus parade. Did I fail to mention you just saved a German village from Apache? They got some of my *raza* along as teamsters and servants, I think, but most of them seem to be just off the boat from some place called Hamburgado."

As if to prove Moreno's point, at least two dozen folk came over the crest at them, jawing in their own guttural lingo about something. Most were men. The others were women and children. From the way they were all beaming at him he suspected they'd just nominated him for sainthood, if not the presidency.

There was one blond gal he'd have nominated for most anything she might ever hanker to be. He sized her up as somewhere in her early twenties, a mite tall for her age, the way so many Viking princesses seemed to sprout. After that her big blue eyes matched the checks on her gingham dress as she stared at him right adoringsome.

But it seemed they'd elected a way uglier sight to speak for all of them. Whether he was their boss or just the one who spoke Spanish the best. He was almost as tall and way fatter than Longarm. He had blue eyes, too, albeit his duds were rumpled white linen and his hair was the color of galvanized wire. He said he was a hairy Kruger and that he and his party were bound for the big copper strike at Santa Rosalia with a mess of fancy German mining machinery.

Longarm was fairly sure he'd heard the cuss right, albeit his Spanish was awful and his words didn't add up right. So Longarm asked if the hairy cuss spoke English.

He didn't. But that bodacious blond gal did, even better than most if one ignored the charming trouble she seemed to have with any words spelled with an R or a W. She said she was Frau Lion Erica Lindermann on her way to join kin in Santa Rosalia.

So Longarm ticked his hat brim to her and explained, "I only know of one important copper mining center called

Santa Rosalia, ma'am. It's over in Baja, California."

She nodded brightly and said, "That is what they told us. That is where we were bound when those horrid Yaqui attacked us about two hours ago. Herr Kruger and these others want me to express their undying gratitude to you and this heroic Mexican cavalier."

Moreno blushed down from his palomino and muttered something under his breath it was just as well nobody heard too clearly.

Longarm shot him a warning look and, turning back to Erica, insisted, "I'm missing something, here, unless it's you folk needing a way better map. Like I just said, Santa Rosalia is over to Baja, California. That's a substantial but separate part of Mexico. It's a peninsula with the Sea of Cortez or Gulf of California separating it from the mainland. Them copper mines you mentioned are about halfway down the Baja, facing this way but across at least a hundred miles of deep sea water!"

She didn't look upset to hear this. She nodded and said, "We shall naturally board a steam ferry at Tiberon, once we've crossed this dreadful wasteland."

Longarm glanced up at Moreno to ask, "Tiberon? Don't that mean the same as shark?"

The Mexican nodded and said, "Is also an island in the Sea of Cortez. Nobody lives there but a few wreckers and pirates, in season. Perhaps is also the name of some seaport I have never heard of, no?"

Erica had been following their confusion. She said, "Of course it is a seaport. How could we reach a desert island from the mainland with all this heavy mining machinery, except by steam ferry? Our guide, Marin, assured us we'd be able to run our freight wagons right on deck from the dock at the town of Tiberon."

Longarm shrugged and said, "A guide would know better than me. Where might this Marin you hired be, ma'am?"

She lowered her eyelids and replied, "Alas, poor Marin was one of the first to fall when those terrible Yaqui ambushed us."

That somehow failed to surprise Longarm as much as it might have. He said, "I figured things were just commencing to go too smooth this morning. Don't tell me you folk were navigating the Sonora Desert with a handy Mex instead of a survey map?"

She said, "Marin said he'd been through this desert many times in the past, at different times of the year."

She waved an expansive hand at the grass, the *dry* grass all around, and added, "That is why he suggested this shortcut, off the usual route but taking advantage of all this fodder for our teams."

Longarm counted under his breath to keep from cussing before he muttered, "I asked you not to tell me that, ma'am. But does anyone ever listen?"

Then he told Moreno, "Fetch me a fresh mount, you otherwise useless *pendejo.* Can't you see we got a lot of exploring ahead of us if we don't aim to run out of water before we figure out where we might be?"

Chapter 12

Despite the grass-covered swells all around, it was getting hot and fixing to get hotter by the time Longarm had taken stock of the situation over by the wagon circle. Another three men had died inside the circle whilst defending it. One woman had blown out her own brains, despite her own homely face, lest those howling Yaqui ravage her fair white body. Four other men in the party had been wounded but figured to live if the water it took to dress their wounds held out as well. They had suicide watches on two gals, one German and one Mex, who'd lost kids as the wagons had been hastily circled. The four gals who'd only lost men would likely get over it in time.

Herr Kruger seemed to think Longarm and Moreno were guides. Longarm didn't argue. He didn't want the friendly but somewhat flustered mining engineer to get them more lost than they were. So, seeing nobody talked back, he directed them to bury their own dead before it got any hotter.

Once they'd done so, and said both some Catholic and Lutheran words over 'em, they left the dead stock and shot-up Indians to those patient buzzards. Longarm didn't let on he had no idea where they all might be. He just said it was best to put some distance between them and all that carnage. For openers, the Indians were sure to return for their own dead if and when they ever caught up with those ponies Longarm had run off.

At the suggestion of a surviving Mex teamster, he'd swapped his bigger *rurale* mount for a spunky but less husky paint one of the dead gents had been riding. The original rider of Moreno's new palomino and charro saddle had been one of the first to fall, which was why they'd encountered the riderless pony to begin with.

The heavier, possibly slower *rurale* stock was more fit to pull carts in place of the mules they'd lost in the attack. That had still left them shy of draft brutes. They'd solved the problem as best they could by abandoning the baggage of the dead, hanging on to their rations and water, of course, and shifting freight about 'til they were able to dispense with three of the smaller carts.

Erica got to ride up front with Herr Kruger in his lead wagon. So Longarm fell in beside them on his new paint, on the blonde's side of course, as they trended more to the northwest than they'd been headed under the guidance of the late Marin Garcia. They didn't argue but of course they wanted to know why.

He explained, "Your guide might have known where he was leading you. I'd rather follow wagon ruts in such treachersome country."

Erica protested, as she gazed about at mostly gentle rises covered with tawny shortgrass, "This country does not look at all treacherous to me, Herr Long. I'll admit it seemed quite sinister to us, coming down through the rocky foothills into what seemed, at first, a jungle of, how do you say it, cactus trees?"

He dryly replied, "They call 'em saguaros in these parts, Miss Erica. I said I savvied why your guide took this shortcut across a less pricklesome *llano*. It ain't the grass all around I'm worried about. It's the lay of the land under it, do we cross her the wrong way. Have you folk ever heard of the Donner Party and the swell shortcut they took through uncharted desert back in '46?"

Erica hadn't. She couldn't have been born that early. But Herr Kruger nodded brightly and exclaimed in his bad Spanish that he'd read indeed about those other Germans bound for the western mining country. He asked if it was true they'd wound up eating one another.

Longarm asked Erica if she spoke Spanish as well. Once she allowed she did, he explained in that tongue to them both, "The Donners were German-American and there's some argument as to who might have eaten whom. They weren't headed for the California goldfields, because nobody had struck gold in California that early. They were simply honest pioneers, looking for new lands to settle in a golden West they'd only heard about."

"What was that about them eating one another?" Erica asked.

He said, "That wasn't their original intent. The story is too long as well as too sad to go into. The only point to remember is that they took a shortcut, far from the beaten track, on the advice of a guide who might or might not have known what he was talking about. He wasn't with them when they got lost. If he had been he might have been able to lead them over the mountains ahead. He wasn't. So they wandered in and out of some blind canyons until, when they did in fact find a pass over the High Sierra it was already October and it snows that early in the snowy saw. They weren't expecting that, either, so . . ."

"Herr Gott! You expect a snowstorm ahead?" demanded Herr Kruger with a nervous laugh.

Longarm wiped at his own sweaty neck with a pocket kerchief as he ruefully replied, "Heatstroke seems more likely this far south. But don't sell the Sonora Desert short when it comes to odd weather. A lot of lost travelers die of thirst around here, it's true. But you'd be surprised how many drown, or get struck by lightning."

Erica glanced up at the cloudless cobalt blue bowl above as she demanded, "What difference could it make if we were out here on this meadowland or following your lost wagon ruts when or if we had a storm like that one we rode through yesterday?"

He soberly said, "A lot of difference, if we were crossing a deep enough playa when it hit. A playa is a harmless-looking stretch of desert that would be a lake, sometimes a mighty big one, in wetter parts of this mostly wet world."

She said she knew what a playa was. He said, "They call rivers as impressive as the wide Missouri arroyos out here, when they have no water between their sometimes steep banks. But flash flooding is only one of the obstacles to travel across country you just don't know. I could list things alphabetical or numerical you'd never get a heavy wagon through or over. Suffice it to say there would be no Camino Diablo to follow if one could just cross this desert any way one might want to wander."

Herr Kruger frowned thoughtfully ahead, beyond his team into the Great Unknown, as he announced, "Before he was killed, Marin told us there was more than one beaten path his people called El Camino Diablo."

Longarm nodded and said, "Almost any one of them ought to do. I know they followed different routes at different times of the year. Like your more recent Marin, the colonial wagon masters must have known of graze and water that would be there, or not there, according to the way the desert winds had been blowing. I know desert Indians wander all over, sometimes where no white would think to wander, in search of flora and fauna few whites, or other Indians, would eat. They say those A-rab sheepherders who graze the Sahara find pasture here one time and somewhere else another. Desert range is like that. My point is that while natives who know a desert can wander far off the beaten path, it's not safe for anyone *else*. I vote we find a well-defined wagon route and follow it west, knowing that sooner or later it has to lead us somewhere."

Herr Kruger agreed. Erica proved how smart she was by asking him, in English, "What if, when we come upon such a trail, this should be the wrong time of the year to follow it? Poor Marin said there would be more water as well as plenty of grazing, back the way he was leading us when we encountered those Yaqui, Herr Long!"

He said, "Let's be fair and call 'em Nadene, or Apache. I know I could use a haircut about now but my friends still call me Custis, Miss Erica."

She looked sort of blank. Then she laughed like hell and passed the joke on to Herr Kruger, in German. So he got to chuckle, too, as she told Longarm, "I was not addressing you as Hair Long, ah, Custis. I was calling you Herr Long, see?"

He said, "Nope. Sounds the same to me, either way." So both Germans got to laugh at him some more.

He said, "Go ahead. We had us some German folk who'd drifted down from Penn State, back in West-By-God-Virginia, and you all can sound sort of comical trying to talk our lingo, you know."

She asked what was wrong with her English. He told her, "Nothing. Your Spanish is better than mine, too. Anyone can tell you studied both in some school. But these squareheads back home used to give us all a good chuckle by saying things like 'Throw the chickens from the shed some feed and also throw the cow over the fence some hay.' "

She didn't get it. She understood those distant German-Americans had made mistakes in English grammar but she didn't picture livestock being flung about the way most English speakers might. He said, "Well, just call me Custis and leave my durned hair out of it."

She arched one blond brow and decided, "You are teasing me, *nicht wahr?*"

So he grinned sheepishly and said, "Yep. I sort of like to tease pretty ladies. I'll cut it out if you'd rather."

She said she didn't mind a little teasing, as long as he didn't get too fresh. When he asked how he'd know if he was getting too fresh, she said she'd let him know.

The ground seemed to be rising a mite as they rolled on, but Lord only knew why they were starting to pass small patches of prickle pear and big patches of bare dirt, now.

Longarm knew greasewood and some of the other stickerbushes of the low chaparral poisoned the soil around 'em so's grass couldn't compete for such water as there might be. But pear and even saguaro fought fair and just grew green and juicy on less water than, say, spinach. Lots of folk throughout the Southwest grew cactus hedges right around their well-watered orchards or gardens. So it was safe to say they were passing less grass, now, just because the ground was getting drier.

Erica was the one with the curiosity to ask. Mining engineers such as ol' Herr Kruger were likely more interested in the bedrock under the surface soil than anything growing up on top of everything. When the German gal asked Longarm if he suspected they were coming on, say, alkali, he shook his head and said, "You see saltbush sprouting where the groundwater's tainted dangerous. Every desert traveler should know what saltbush looks like. I'd be proud to point some out to you if there was any to see. But there ain't. So such water as there is is safe for man or beast."

She asked how poisonous this saltbush of his might be. He smiled grimly and explained, "It ain't poisonous at all. Stock just loves to browse its pleasantly sour leaves and the Indians grind a fair flour from saltbush seeds. That's what makes the stuff so treachersome. I mind this water hole I come upon one time, up in the Mojave, cool and clear in the lee of some rocks with saltbush all around, knee-high and green as emeralds. There was this old sun-silvered prairie schooner parked nearby. The canvas had rotted and blown away. The team that had hauled it that far was reduced to chalky piles of bones. The folk who'd been riding in the wagon, all the way from Lord-knows-where, weren't in much better shape. Being from other parts, wherever they'd come from, they hadn't known saltbush grows best where nothing else can. The water in that desert spring was likely laced with lead and arsenic. Them pioneers and their stock might never have drunk enough to kill 'em then and there if the water had been tainted with regular sea salts."

Erica repressed a shudder and passed it on to Herr Kruger in German. He just shrugged and told them both in Spanish that he'd heard about all the chlorides of arsenic, lead, and what all you had to watch for in hardrock mining country.

Juan Moreno rode up the wagon train on his palomino to fall in beside Longarm as he asked, too worried to cuss, "For why are you leading us to the northwest into so much cactus? The teamster of my *raza* seem most upset. They say their old leader, Marin Garcia, told them the cutoff they were following would take them to that coastal village with plenty of grass and water every other day."

Longarm shrugged and replied, "*Quien sabe?* Do I look like a dead Mexican? When you don't know where you are or where you're going you look for a signpost or, failing that, a beaten path that seems to lead somewhere more sensible."

Moreno tried, "Just rolling the way they were going would take us sooner or later to the sea, no?"

Longarm grimaced and asked, "What do you call that Mex canyon deeper and wider than the more famous Grand Canyon up Arizona way?"

Moreno said, "I know the one you mean. I forget what they call it. Few have ever see it because it runs through arid unsettled range and . . . I see what you mean."

Longarm nodded and said, "*Bueno.* Tell your *paisanos* any one of 'em who can draw me a map of that dead teamster's cutoff is welcome to play Moses in the Wilderness. Otherwise, we'd best stick to less imaginative navigation."

"*Pero* Brazo Largo . . ." the young Mex began, only to have Longarm cut him off with, "*Pero* me no *peros* and but me no buts, for that matter. We got us a whole herd of livestock along with a heap of men, women, and children that'll never last more than a day or so on such water as we seem to be hauling. El Camino Diablo, wherever in tarnation it might be, was laid out by old timers who knew how to get across this dry country alive. Draft stock can haul farther hungry than thirsty. But there could be further advantages in sticking to the tried and true ruts in less appealing country.

It might not appeal to those Nadene raiders once they catch up with their own stock."

Moreno nodded soberly and said, "*Es verdad*. Now you are starting to make sense."

Chapter 13

Over to the southeast, on the far side of that temporary lake and ageless lava flat, the leader of a long and dusty cavalry column raised his free gauntlet and reined in his cream Arab as he spied two of his mounted scouts frogmarching an Indian on foot his way. The seminaked savage was a peaceful Pima, from the look of his hairdo and footgear. El Presidente had issued standing orders not to upset the Pima or Papago needlessly. The dictatorship was having enough trouble with Yaqui and Chihuahua at the moment and, while the pedestrian tribes of the Sonora Desert seldom bothered anyone without provocation, they could fight like demons from Hell when provoked.

Pima and Papago both made war with the same dogged determination they scoured the desert for food and water when common sense said they'd find neither. Tales were told of mounted Apache raiders being followed, on foot, all the way back to the White Mountains north of the border to be butchered in their beds in the dead of night by the simple food gatherers they'd despised. The Yaqui hadn't bothered them in living memory. Some said it was because they spoke the same tongue. Others said it simply proved how smart as well as vicious the Yaqui could be.

The Mexican cavalry leader called out to his scouts, "Show more *cortesía* to our *amigo Indio, soldados.*"

As they reined in to let the Pima walk for himself, the cavalry leader saw he was a wiry middle-aged man with one good eye. The mestizo officer was joined by a full-blooded corporal fluent in Classic Nahuatl as the older Indian came within conversational range. The officer ordered his translator to question the Pima. When the corporal tried, the Pima sneered, in Spanish, "You speak Ho like a cactus wren being devoured by ants. Do I look like one of those *mariposas* from the central highlands?"

The Mexican officer laughed and said, "We are searching for Yaqui from the mountains between here and there, *viejo*. Would you care for some tobacco?"

The Pima grimaced and said, "*Ka!* I have not come all this way to beg crumbs from *saltu* I care nothing about."

One of the scouts who'd frogmarched him many a *vara* snorted and told his superior, "He did not come to anyone, *mayor mío!* We caught the old *cabrón* and brought him to you."

Their leader growled, "*Silencío.* I tend to believe he came to us of his own free will. I have had some experience in tracking wild ones in their own chaparral."

Turning back to the Indian, he asked more politely what a fellow citizen of Los Estados Unidos de Mejico might have in mind.

The Pima said, "Some *chicas cagadas* of my band think they are so big. They returned to our *rancherita* with fan palm fruit and a tale of *saltu* lovers who possessed bigger *pitóns* than any *hombre* of our *raza!*"

The officer murmured, "*Saltu . . .* ?" and his translator murmured back, "Strangers, *Mayor mío.*"

The officer nodded in understanding and said, "Women who taunted the men of my old neighborhood with something like that would wind up with the mark of the cow carved across their fresh faces."

The Pima shrugged and said, "We do not punish women for doing what comes naturally to their weaker natures. Men are supposed to use more self-control, unless they wish for to die young. I was out looking for those *saltu* who made love to *muchachas, two muchachas,* who'd told me I was too old and ugly. I had just cut their trail when I saw these riders scouting for you and decided to let you kill them *for* me. I am very brave as well as most insulted, *pero* there are two of them and as you see I have no gun."

The Mexican officer laughed and said, "Remind me never to flirt with a *muchacha* who shows no respect for her elders, *viejo.* But for why should La Caballeria Federale go to that much trouble over your unhappy love life? We are out after Yaqui, not wandering *vaqueros* who trifle with other men's *mujeres."*

The Pima smiled slyly and insisted, "I think you would be interested in *these* two *saltu.* One is of your *raza, pero* a *bandido* of some kind, according to those shameless *muchachas* who boast of his *pitón.* The other was, how you say, gringo? Anyway, the *muchachas* they had so much fun with said they were worried about *los rurales* and, oh yes, they had five or six *caballos* carrying *rurale* harness and brands!"

The officer blinked, turned to the subordinate to his left and asked, "Do you still have that *telegrama* from *los rurales, lugarteniente?"*

The junior officer replied, "Alas, no, *pero* I recall what it said about that notorious gringo, El Brazo Largo, and something about a wanted *bandido* he stole from them, again."

The major nodded curtly and decided, "They were right to suspect El Brazo Largo of ambushing those *rurales* over to the northeast if he and his prisoner are traveling with *rurale* mounts."

The Indian had been listening. He piped up, "There were some other *rurales* through here ahead of you. I can put you on to their trail, as well, if you like."

The cavalry leader shook his head and said, "They have not sent us out after *los rurales.* Come to think of it, they did not order us to bring in El Brazo Largo, either. But somehow I feel there may be a medal in it for me if I do. So why don't you show us to the trail of these, ah, *saltu* you are so annoyed with, *viejo."*

The old Pima nodded, eagerly, and said, "Follow me. I can show you where they parted company from those *chicas malvadas*. If you can not follow such a clear trail from there you have no business this far from your mother's side!"

Chapter 14

By noon it was hot as the hinges of hell and that many hooves and wagon wheels raised an awesome amount of dust as they busted through caliche. That patch of *llano* lost in the desert had been left far behind and they were back in cactus country. The German folk had heard about barrel cactus, called *bisaga* by Mexicans and nigger heads by unreconstructed Texicans, and seemed to think that's what the tall saguaro all about might be. When Erica asked how one went about tapping a famous barrel cactus for all that water stored inside, Longarm had to laugh before he explained, "You don't. *Bisaga* would be called pot cactus if early Anglo travelers had been paying more attention, Miss Erica. The Mexicans make cactus candy by boiling strips of *bisaga* a spell in the sweeter juice of *nopal* or saguaro fruit with mayhaps some store-bought sugar. The Indians are inclined to use a handy so-called barrel cactus as a cooking pot."

"You are teasing me again," she insisted.

He said, "Nope. It's pure fact. They cut off the top of a *bisaga*. It would tip over if they cut it off at the roots. Then they scoop it hollow and strain the pulp to pour the greenish but fairly tasteless juice back in. Sometimes they add broth or even more water, but there's generally enough natural juice to fill the pot once they've added the jerked meat, mesquite beans, parched corn, and such."

"You mean they make some sort of cold stew in tepid cactus juice?"

"Not hardly. That'd taste disgusting. You got to boil jerked meat and mummified vegetables a long time to get 'em edible. I know it sounds impossible. It sounded wild to me, the first time a mountain man told me about brewing coffee in a birch bark cone. But Indians had to figure out how to cook before they saw the first iron pot, or even a clay one. Most who know how to bake pottery don't risk it over a fire, full of cold water. They boil water by dropping hot rocks in it. Rocks get mighty hot, setting amid hardwood coals, and they don't have no taste of their own, of course, so . . ."

"*Ach,* there is in my homeland a brewery that drops white-hot stones in its mash instead of boiling it!" she cut in, adding, "They call the results *steinbier* or stone beer."

Longarm licked his dry lips and said, "Sounds a mite odd, but I wish I had some right now. Getting back to barrel cactus, so's we can sort of forget it, it's only a cactus as grows in a handy shape. You can get a slightly green and sticky substitute for canteen water out of most any cactus. Some tastes soapier or slimier than others, but none of it will hurt you half as much as going thirsty in this dry heat."

As they topped a slight rise Herr Kruger, on the blonde's far side, muttered, "*Ach, wohin jetzt?*" and Longarm didn't really need Erica's polite translation. He wasn't sure which way they ought to swing, either, as he stared soberly ahead into prickle pear, a heap of prickle pear, stretching smack across their path in both directions, far as the eye could see.

As they reined in to study all that thorny greenery Longarm calmly announced, "That's what we call a pear flat. The soil in these parts must suit the roots of *nopal* as exceedingly as that soil back yonder encouraged shortgrass. Saguaro likes to stand aloof, and cholla, praise the Lord, seldom grows so close together. *Nopal*, or prickle pear, seems to think it's an infernal hedge plant. You seldom see *that* much of in one big bunch, though!"

Erica said she was glad and asked which way might be best to drive around it. He blinked and asked why in thunder they'd want to do that.

Then Moreno and a dozen other Mexicans rode by, yipping joyfully as a pack of alley curs who'd just spied a bitch in heat. A couple already had their machetes drawn and waving.

Longarm told the bemused Germans, "It's already past siesta time on a day like today and next to a watered canyon shaded with willow you ain't about to find a better place to shade and water than a pear flat. It gives us a swell edge on them Indians we brushed with back on that *llano* or, knock wood, any others sneaking about in these parts."

Erica tried to translate his English explanation into German to Herr Kruger. But she didn't really follow Longarm's drift 'til they got closer and she could see what their Mex help was up to.

A human afoot or even on horseback could work well into if not through a pear flat, winding about as much as a kid in one of those garden mazes rich folk planted back East for some fool reason. But the thorny pads seldom left space to drive even a two-wheel cart, let alone a longer, lumbering freight wagon.

Fortunately, although protected from the muzzles of browsing stock by rosettes of needle-sharp spines, the green lollipop pads sliced like bread, or maybe watermelon rind, no matter where a machete blade might hit it, high or low.

Once they'd carved their way in a few yards, afoot, the skilled machete swingers found some growth towering as high as eight or ten feet. They wisely spared as much of that as possible, carving lanes and bays not much wider than the canvas-covered carts and wagons. No draft critter raised in Sonora would have to be taught that cactus stubs cut below the level of any thorny pads made juicy graze in place, albeit the mules and ponies had an edge, with their buckteeth, on the oxen. Way more than all the stock could consume in the time they'd have lay piled to one side for each teamster, or better yet the kids, to peel and feed to the stock like flat green apples. The *mujeres* would chop up choicer pads for nopal salad to go with their late dinner or early supper of tortillas and beans. Erica said she'd already noticed the way folk living in such a climate liked to space out five or six small meals instead of two or three heavy ones like folk off cooler spreads.

Whacking out all that squishy cactus had left the resultant shady lanes smelling more like tossed lettuce or a fresh-cut lawn than before, albeit there was still a tang in the air to identify the place as Old Mexico. As soon as things commenced to get organized well inside the cactus patch, Longarm took Moreno aside, where the dusty gap between the thorny pads was natural, to say, "We got to talk, Juan. I can't say you've been doing anything wrong since we joined up with this party but I don't recall anyone putting you in charge of all them other Mexicans."

Moreno shrugged and said, "*Somebody* had to tell them what to do. They seemed lost without their old *jiba*. I think he told them when to *chinga* and where to *cagada*. None of these *chingado* Germans has told them to do anything. If you would rather appoint some other *cabrón* as your *segundo*, go ahead. I never said I was bigger than *you*, did I?"

Longarm smiled thinly and replied, "Just so we've got that straight. Laying all my cards on the table, I'll allow it occurred to me a gent getting thick with a crowd headed for the Baja might have second thoughts about coming events up Denver way."

Moreno smiled boyishly and replied, "If you would like for to see some cards on the table the thought has crossed my mind, more than once. I have had plenty of chances for to give you the slip, if I really wanted to, no?"

Longarm dryly observed, "I'll be the judge of that. You may have noticed it's easier to *run* than it might be to *hide*."

Moreno nodded soberly and said, "*Es verdad,* I am tired of both. You say that if I am not the greaser who robbed that train I have nothing to fear from a gringo judge and jury. I have never been to your estado Colorado. I think I can prove that to even a gringo's satisfaction. Once I do, I shall be free for to walk out of your Denver *cortejo* a free man, wanted nowhere in Los Estados Unidos del Norte, eh?"

"You'll still be wanted here in Mexico," Longarm began. Then he smiled sheepishly and said, "I follow your drift. It would be sort of stupid to leap from such a friendly frying pan into an even hotter fire, wouldn't it?"

Moreno said, "What really convinced me was your friendship with that rebel leader, El Gato. Is possible for to avoid *los rurales*. It may be possible for to hide from El Brazo Largo in my own country. *Pero* is impossible for to hide from so many on both sides of the law as well as the border and, you will see, I never robbed no *chingado* train north of the *chingado* border!"

Longarm reached for some smokes, noted he was down to the last of those cheroots, and handed the Mex a *claro* instead, as he said, "I'm glad we're straight on that. Getting back to how we mean to get back to Denver alive, and seeing you got the boys listening to you, I'd like at least half a dozen old boys out on perimeter guard at all times as long as we're here. Nobody can see us shading here amid all this *nopal*, but it works both ways. A Nadene or Yaqui could be standing close enough to hear our every word just a few yards off and we'd never notice 'til he joined in. We left a broad, clear trail across the caliche, getting here, and . . ."

"*Mierda*, is already taken care of," Moreno cut in, adding, "I said I never robbed that train. I never said I was a *mariposa* who had never dodged *rurales* or any other *raza* of savage riders. I posted eight, with their guns, a rifle shot out in every direction. Let me worry about it. Did you think I robbed trains with Apache or Yaqui?"

Longarm laughed and said, "That makes it official. Should anyone ask, you're my *segundo* in charge of *seguridad*. That's providing I can get Herr Kruger to let us act so uppity. It's his party when you get right down to brass tacks and I don't recall him inviting us to take charge."

Moreno shrugged and said, "That is for why I started telling his lost sheep what to do. As I just told you, he seems incapable of giving orders. Maybe he knows more about digging copper than getting there for to dig it, eh?"

Longarm agreed that seemed about the size of it, but added, "He's still paying the piper. So he gets to call the tune when and if he cares to. See you don't forget that as you swagger about, *Segundo*."

Moreno chuckled and said, "You noticed the young widows I have been doing my best for to console, eh? Speaking of consoling, is cool as it ever gets in Sonora at siesta time, under a wagon bed surrounded by *nopal*, and we got, what, four hours at least for to *buscar unas mamitas*?"

Longarm said, "*Buscar* all you like but don't take off your pants without making sure nobody's sneaking up on us. I ain't interested in consoling any widow I've noticed, so far."

Moreno shrugged and said, "*Mierda,* what is a little mustache as long as she got *la figura de la primera*? You want the younger one? She's not bad, if you don't mind a flat chest and a skinny *culo*. I think she likes you. She asked me if I thought you were after that big German *puta*."

Longarm frowned and said, "Watch your mouth, *pendejo*. The lady you're talking about is a lady and you can tell your Mex *putas* I just said so!"

"*Ay, que romántico!*" The Mexican laughed, adding, "I did not think you two had advanced to defending one another's good names, yet. *Pero* where might your big, blond *querida* be at siesta time if you are so fond of her, eh?"

Longarm laughed despite himself and said, "Taking her siesta, most likely. I was too polite to ask whether she bunks in Herr Kruger's wagon or elsewhere."

Moreno stated, flatly, "She sleeps in her own two-wheeler, along with a houseful of *mierda por la dote* she has been hauling all the way from her own country for to marry some *hombre* in Santa Rosalia."

Longarm didn't ask how a Mex gossiping with spitesome sounding *mujeres* might have learned so much about Erica Lindermann. He tried to ignore the sour taste his cheroot had turned as he growled, "I reckon a lady has the right to marry up with anyone she wants. Meanwhile there's no saying just how long we'll be riding with this outfit so why don't you just run along and console both those gossips for all I care?"

Moreno said he'd do his best and added a suggestion as to how that sounded like fun, in its own dirty way. As the randy young Mex commenced to turn away he slyly added, "None of us will be seeing much of one another, ever again, once we have for to say *adiós* on this side of the Sea of Cortez, eh?"

Longarm nodded and agreed, "I don't see you and me hopping a steam ferry across to Santa Rosalia. Once we hit the coast trail north to the Colorado Delta and the border just beyond, your wicked widows will be no more than pleasant memories, and vice versa."

"My point exactly," Moreno pointed out, adding, "They say that big one is on her way to join an older *hombre* she has not seen since she was no more than nine or ten, and still a virgin, back in Germany."

Longarm whistled softly and said, "I should hope so. Them *mujeres* you've been gossiping with sure seem to know a lot, for hired help!"

Moreno shrugged and said, "It is the flat-chested one who likes you she talks to. None of them can keep their *bocas* shut when they are having their hair done, eh? The *chica* you are too proud to console was afraid her *patrona* would grasp at the chance for to have a little fun before she settles down in Santa Rosalia as the young *mujer* of a fat old mine supervisor."

Longarm snorted in disgust and said, "Well, I can see your informant wasn't no virgin when *she* married young."

Moreno laughed and said, "I wish I had a *centavo* for every old man who thinks he's getting a virgin. I would never have to rob trains again. Would you like to hear about the German cavalry officer one ran off with when she was sixteen?"

Longarm snapped, "Nope. The lady's past ain't none of my infernal beeswax and that *puta* she confided in should be ashamed."

Moreno shrugged and asked, *"Por que?* She was not the one who ran away with an *hombre* her family did not approve of. Then there was this handsome merchant marine officer, aboard the steamer her stern parents marched her aboard for to join her intended, here in this less Protestant country . . ."

Longarm snapped, "Ay, *callate la trompa!* I mean it! Don't go passing such *mierda* on, neither, lest you find out what they mean about the open mouth attracting flies!"

"Ay, que romántico! I'd better get out of here before someone challenges me to an affair of honor!" laughed the informative young cuss as Longarm stomped off through the cactus jungle, more informed about Erica Lindermann than he felt comfortable with.

He knew there was no decent way to tell a lady she shouldn't confide her darker secrets to a flighty and likely jealous servant. But should the same sort of gossip get back to the man she was on her way to wed, after she'd wed him . . .

"It's none of our beeswax and hardly a federal offense," he muttered under his breath as he gripped the cheroot in his teeth to unbutton his fly in the privacy of a secluded clearing, he thought.

He'd watered a cactus good, shaken the dew from his lily, and was standing there with his semi-erection still in hand when Erica Lindermann busted through the prickle pear at him, all red-faced, to blurt, "I'm going to murder that silly Ynez! But first let me explain!"

Then she blushed even redder as she spied what Longarm was trying to shove back inside his pants before she could spy it. He expected her to turn away and bolt. That's what *he* usually did when he opened the door of a crapper to spy someone already in there. But she only turned the back of her blue-checked summer frock on him so's he could recover some damned dignity as she sobbed, "It sounds so sordid, retold in jest with a Spanish accent! But I am not the *hure* you take me for! I'm not! *Wirlklich* I'm not! I was really in love with Horst and as for that first mate, well, a healthy young woman has needs and it is all too true I am on my way to a man old enough to be my father!"

Having buttoned his fly and disposed of his smoke, Longarm moved closer to soothe, "I know all about needs, ma'am, and I wouldn't worry about old men if I was pretty as you. It'll likely all work out for the best, in Santa Rosalia. But since we just now established how easy it might be for others to overhear our private conversations, I'd get rid of that Ynez and watch what I said to her replacement if I was having my own hair done so often."

She turned around but couldn't seem to meet his gaze as she sighed and said, "I'm not as worried about the servants talking as I am you men! I was on my way to invite you for some tea and pastry when I overheard how nasty you men could make a few little indiscretions sound!"

Longarm soberly replied, "If you were listening careful you never heard me say anything nasty about you, Miss Lindermann."

She dimpled at him shyly and said, "Please call me Erica. You were very sweet about it, as a matter of fact. But now I suppose I am going to have to be very sweet to you, if I expect you to keep my little secrets?"

Longarm started to protest he was a lawman, not an infernal blackmailer who'd take advantage of a lady just because she was a beautiful blonde and he had something on her. But then he wondered why anyone might want to say a dumb thing like that. So he said, "I ain't sure we ought to enjoy tea and other pleasures back at your cart, ah, Erica. Be more private if we was to carry on the rest of this conversation off in the cactus a ways, see?"

She glanced down as she mused, "Without so much as a picnic cloth? *Ach,* I see what you mean. That sand does seem clean and dry as well as cool and shady, *nicht wahr*?"

So they headed off through some narrow gaps and it was her notion to whirl and plant a moist, hungry kiss on him before they'd gone too far.

He kissed back with as much enthusiasm as most men would have, but as she commenced to sort of slide down him to the sand he hung on long enough to say, "You know how much I want you, seeing you've been wanted this way in your time, but I'd never be able to face myself in the shaving mirror again if I thought I was getting you just to keep me from blabbing dirty about you."

She sighed and asked, "Does that mean you won't tell anyone about this tiny bit of pleasure we're stealing from eternity, *liebehaber*?"

So, seeing it seemed mutual, he let his own knees buckle and they started out with only his hat and gunbelt and her skirts out of the way. But once she'd observed and he'd agreed it was a tad warm, even in the shade, to really get at it with their duds on, he shucked everything but his socks, stripped her down to her high button shoes and silk stockings, and started over from scratch, her frilly garters scratching his bare flanks, on top of her spread-out frock.

She sure was tight and put together firm for such a big, buxom blonde. She knew how grand she looked bare by broad day as well and seemed to enjoy the way he admired all of her, from aloft on locked elbows, as they both watched it sliding in and out of the blond thatch between her wide-spread creamy thighs.

As they shared a cigar, he was out of cheroots, to see if they could get their second winds, Erica commenced to tell him why she'd been so wicked with cavalry officers, steamship mates and such. He told her he wished women wouldn't do that, adding, "You don't see *me* confessing every damned dance with the girls I left behind me in West-By-God-Virginia. I just know you screwed silly, and vice versa, because it feels so damned nice, not because my elders made me dance with an ugly schoolmarm to be polite or because I'd rather stick my old organ grinder in an ugly schoolmarm than say a pencil sharpener!"

She took the cigar from her smiling lips as she demanded, "Why, Custis, did you really make love to that ugly school teacher your parents demanded you dance with?"

He smiled sheepishly and said, "Sure I did. The poor old gal didn't really want to dance as much as she wanted to screw. We did it way later, after the barn dance, of course. My point is that I doubt she ever told any other gents about the overgrown pupil she made hot, fevered love to after midnight, in the schoolyard. She was a good old gal who just plain *liked* what you said about stealing a bit of forever from the cruel jaws of Time. If she's still alive she must be getting on by now, but that one little slice of pure pleasure we tore off that night was worth every grass stain and grunt it cost us."

Erica placed the cigar back between his lips and commenced to kiss his bare flesh as she crooned, "I feel sure I know just how she must have felt. Were you this big, all over, when you were a schoolboy?"

He said, "Nope. I've grown some, since. But it evens out. She said she hadn't had much experience, old as she was by the time I had what I had to give her in her. You see, she'd been sort of watching me and the other older boys grow up and, well, I reckon I'd grown big enough by that night she went loco all of a sudden."

Then he laughed like hell as he realized what he'd been doing and said, "I'll be switched with snakes if I ain't confessing my *own* weak-natured ways to another gal who wasn't there and couldn't care less! Do you find it interesting that the first schoolmarm I ever trifled with had sort of pruney lips but real swell nipples, Erica?"

She grimaced and said, "No. I'm not sure I'd like to picture you kissing either, now that you mention it."

He nodded and said, "That's why you ought to quit telling the man you're with about men you've been with before. I don't mind you knowing how to screw so grand, in the abstract. But I'd just as soon not picture the way or ways you learned, in detail."

She didn't answer. Her puckered pink lips were busy with pleasures more enjoyable than gossip. He was glad, as he lay back to blow smoke rings as she blew him. For it might not have felt half so beautiful if he'd been able to picture her doing that to some other son of a bitch.

She'd obviously done it to someone, more than once, to get that good at it.

Chapter 15

Cutting cactus pads in the shade of others was hot and sweaty, albeit endurable. So once he'd cleared it with the old German boys who were paying the piper, Longarm put a crew to work around two in the afternoon so's they could punch their way out the far side of that big pear flat as soon as they might be safe from sunstroke.

The *muchachos* cut the last pear a little after three-thirty and a Mex could hardly argue siesta time wasn't about over. So they forged on to the northwest across sun-baked caliche too dry for prickle pear, which was mighty dry. The greasewood, chamisa, and such grew in dusty, scattered clumps and the few saguaro looked as if they were fixing to faint. There was still enough cover for serious Indians, though, so Longarm rode a couple of rifle shots out ahead on point with Moreno and a *vaquero* called Chancero scouting along the horizon to either flank.

They'd moved on some and the shadows were getting longer when Longarm heard hoofbeats overtaking him and turned in the saddle to see it was Erica Lindermann riding sidesaddle on her own chestnut barb. She'd changed to a fresh polka dot frock and combed all that dust out of her golden hair, Lord love her. But Longarm still said, "Howdy, honey. I know what you're thinking. It's been a spell. But we'd still better hold the thought until the next trail break."

She pouted a bee stung lower lip at him and demanded, "Is that all you ever think of? Don't you feel like, *ach*, just *talking* to me when you're not sticking that old *thing* in me?"

Longarm rolled his eyes heavenward, feeling mighty sorry as well as just a tad jealous toward that squarehead waiting for all this confusion in Santa Rosalia. Out loud, he said, "Well, sure I like to talk to you, doll face. What would you like to talk about?"

She said, "About us."

He'd been afraid she might. He stared off to the heat-hazed north and soberly said, "There ain't no us to talk about if you're talking about after we're all out of this desert. I told you as we were stealing that tiny bit of eternity back yonder that I'm a worthless cuss with a tumbleweed job and no desire to leave young widows weeping over my likely early grave."

She smiled bitterly and insisted, "I am not asking you to marry me, Custis."

He looked relieved and said, "*Bueno*. The pension they give a deputy marshal's widow is a national disgrace. Come sundown we'll be pausing long enough to sup and let the moon rise. The moon's been waxing and rising twenty minutes earlier every night, but I reckon we might be able to manage a quickie, out behind some greasewood or whatever."

She giggled and said she meant to hold him to that offer. Then she sobered and said, "Custis, I don't want to go to Santa Rosalia. I want to go on up to your country with you and Herr Moreno."

Longarm scowled and muttered, half to himself, "Have you ever had the feeling you were talking to a mighty pretty window dummy? I just now told you, Erica, I don't stay put in one place long enough to matter! Soon as Moreno and me get near a railroad train north of the border we'll be boarding her, no matter which way she may be heading. Once we're well clear of the border and some other worthless rascals we got to beeline up to Denver by passenger coach or freight car. Marshal Billy Vail don't care."

She said, "I have heard your Denver is most *Gemutlichkeit*. I would not care how we might get there."

Longarm hesitated. There was just no saying how many good times they might have left if he didn't piss her off total. But a man had to do what a man had to do so he told her, simply, "I don't stay long between jobs in Denver. When I'm there I got me a dinky hired room on the unfashionsome side of Cherry Creek and my landlady says I don't pay her enough to board anyone else upstairs with me."

She said she was thinking more along the lines of her own place.

He said, "You'd want to look for a job, first. Rents are way higher in Denver than in Santa Rosalia or, heck, Tucson. It ain't that I'm tightfisted with my pals, doll face, but I just don't make enough to keep a gal on the side and if I did . . . You might as well know, I already got me some gals up Denver way and they're all self-supporting, bless their little hearts."

Erica's voice only cooled eight or ten degrees as she insisted, "Neither of us hatched innocent from the egg just before we agreed to be friends back there in that cactus patch. Dammit, Custis, I don't want to be your wife. I don't want to be your mistress. I only want to be an American girl who is free to choose instead of the wife of an old, gray German my elders chose for me! Take me with you, just to the border, if you don't want to make your lovers in Denver jealous. Can't you do that much for me? After all, you know how much I like to do for you, and . . ."

"We'll study on it," he cut in, partly because her offer was so tempting and partly because he'd just glimpsed a different shade of dirt through a gap in the chaparral ahead.

Standing in the stirrups as they rode on, he told her, "Wagon trace, cutting across all this barren waste from northeast to southwest. If it ain't the one and original El Camino Diablo it'll do 'til the right one comes along."

They rode out on the dusty roadway and reined in to await the others. As she stared down the ruts toward the late afternoon sun Erica asked how there could be any doubt which road to the coast they'd stumbled on.

He explained, "This stretch don't look so well beat. Them ruts are clear enough for a blind man with a cane to follow, likely somewhere more important. But once you study on 'em they're little more than breaks in the original crust. No telling how long it's been since last a wagon train rolled through these parts. Meanwhile, one good-sized wagon train could account for the whole shebang and I think I already told you how that Donner Party lit out across uncharted waste on a bum steer."

The blonde regarded the mysterious road to somewhere with less enthusiasm as she asked, "Might it not be wiser to keep going until we come upon the deeper ruts you say you were following before?"

Longarm said, "I'm studying. There's no saying how much further north that might take us and some of your teamsters seem mighty sure your dead guide was aiming farther south. Aside from which, this wagon trace may be the best one, or even the only one."

She said it seemed to her he was only guessing. He told her she was right, explaining, "Guesses is all you got to go on when you just don't know."

He twisted in his saddle to stare back across the low chaparral at the distant wagons, their canvas tops commencing to go from dirty canvas to vanilla frosting in the kinder light of the low-slung sun. He decided, "We can't roll all that far before sundown once they catch up to us, here. Might be best to circle most of the party here for a spell whilst Moreno and me scout forward a few hours ride. It don't take a genius or even a full moon to find a public highway punched through chaparral."

Then old Chancero, way off to the east, fired his saddle gun for attention. Longarm waved his own hat to let the distant *vaquero* know he was interested as he tried to determine why he ought to be. Then he saw why, farther to his left than he'd expected. The puffs of smoke were rising in dotted lines of four, salmon pink against the purple eastern sky, with longer pauses between bursts. There was nothing wrong with Erica's big blue eyes. When she asked him what they were looking at he quietly answered, "Smoke talk. Can't say whether it's Nadene or Yaqui. Most Indians set great store by the number four."

She said, *"Ach,* I have heard of the smoke signals of your Red Indianers. Do you know what they are saying?"

To which he could only reply, "Do I look like a Red Indianer? Even if I was, smoke talk ain't sent in an alphabeticsome code like Morse. They agree on prearranged signals before they split into separate hunting or war parties. Sometimes they don't even want others who talk the same lingo following their drift."

She insisted, "They have to be signaling something about somebody, *nicht wahr?"*

He nodded and said, "Yep. Let's hope it ain't us or, that if it's us, them's Nadene and not Yaqui over yonder."

By this time, as Longarm and the big blonde waited on the wagons, that cavalry column had come upon the remains of those *rurales* El Brazo Largo or in point of fact his prisoner had killed between that flooded playa and the ancient lava damming all that tepid muddy runoff. The cavalry troopers were not pleased. Longarm and Moreno had treated the dead *rurales* with more respect than they'd have likely received from their government in the end. They'd simply left the sons of bitches where they lay. The flood water had receded enough to leave all three spread out on dry caliche. Coyotes had been at them the night before and buzzards had cleaned up most of the good parts since dawn, leaving everything that wasn't a red ruin whitewashed with chalky buzzard shit.

The hard-eyed major in command didn't think he needed the services of a medical examiner to determine the probable causes. One of his sharper troopers had spied spent brass in the slanting sunlight and brought it right over. As the officer examined the empty cartridge cases he decided, "Fired within no more than a few days and they say El Brazo Largo loads both his saddle gun and side arm with this same brand of .44-40 ammunition."

Another trooper approached, afoot, to salute and report, "Someone was chained or perhaps handcuffed to a smoke-tree over that way, *Mayor mío*. I do not understand why, *pero* the cuts in the bark read no other way."

The cavalry leader smiled thinly and said, "I was wondering how that gringo *chingado* got the drop on three grown *rurales*, as good as he is said to be. We know he ran off with that rebel we had the first claim on. He used what's-his-name, Moreno, as bait. He chained him where *los rurales* would hear his bleating, as one stakes out a goat for to nail a *puma* that has been raiding stock."

A junior officer sitting his own mount nearby grimaced and opined, "El Brazo Largo is not so good, just treacherous. Had he faced up to our three boys *mano a mano* I feel sure they'd have beaten him."

The major didn't answer. Junior officers were always saying things like that. A mestizo sergeant who'd won his stripes by taking gross advantage of some Chihuahua raiders in his time called out from atop the leatherlike folds of lava to the west, "*Aquí, Mayor mío!* Steel shod hooves have been over this lava, not too long ago! The scrape marks show no signs of rust and was only the other night we had much rain over this way, no?"

The cavalry leader said a dreadful thing about Longarm's mother and added, "Hard on horses as well as treacherous. *Esta bien,* we can take our own mounts anywhere that *yanqui malo* can. Everyone mount up and follow me up and over this lava *chingado!*"

His second in command hesitated, then called out, "Meaning nothing but the utmost respect, *Mayor mío,* did not our orders read we were to seek out and destroy those Yaqui? *Sin duda* I am mistaken, *pero* I recall nothing about chasing gringos *malos.*"

The major started to call his second in command a *maricon cobarde* but he hadn't gotten to be a field grade officer in a very macho outfit by calling armed and dangerous men cowardly. So he took a deep breath, let it out, and decided, "*Quien sabe?* Perhaps we can finish off both. Meanwhile, you have a point and it might be best to inform Ciudad Mejico we have cut the trail of El Brazo Largo. I wish for you to send a written report back along our trail by dispatch rider. Perhaps you'd better send a full squad for to make sure our message gets through. Headquarters will want to put our report out on the wire in all directions. That way, even if *we* don't catch up with that gringo *chingado* and his prisoner *somebody* on our side will be certain to!"

Chapter 16

Herr Kruger and the others had spied the smoke talk by the time they made it to that unmarked road to anywhere. Before they could bolt off to the west along it Longarm calmed everyone down, or at least shut 'em up, by rising tall in his stirrups to announce, "That ain't the way you get through the dark of the moon in Indian country, gents. The Nadene, or Apache, are notorious night fighters and Yaqui make Nadene look like kids raiding an apple orchard after dark. We don't know for certain we're the object of all that smoke talk. If we are they'll surely circle wide to set up an ambush down the trail ahead. Our best bet's a fort-up with the wagons circled tighter than you had 'em before. We'll want stores and in a pinch chaparral and loose dirt piled at least axle high under every cart and wagon, with a field of fire cleared at least a hundred yards out and . . ."

"We have it on good authority that Red Indianers do not at night attack!" piped up a damned German who read too much English for his own good.

Longarm was too polite to call him an asshole. He suspected he knew the asshole who'd written that down to confuse posterity. He said, "I enjoy them tales Ned Buntline writes about Buffalo Bill as well as the next one. But I don't know where he got that whopper about Indians being afraid of the dark. It's true nobody mounts a cavalry charge in pitch darkness. Look what happened to that light brigade in broad daylight back in '54. But neither Nadene nor Yaqui fight on horseback if they can avoid it. Yaqui in particular like to slither like snakes through the chaparral after dark. That's why we'll want every twig cleared away within rapid fire range and, should any of the reptilian rascals make her as far as our wagon circle, that's why we want to give 'em a rampart of loose dirt and stickerbush to slither through."

Some of 'em passed his suggestions on, in German, to the even more helpless greenhorns. When he saw nobody wanted to argue with that much of his plan he nodded curtly and said, "After that we'll want piles of dry brush, sprinkled with coal oil, laced with black powder and fused with quick-fuse from your mining supplies to flare up, sort of strategic, where they'll outline them instead of us."

For greenhorns, they seemed to catch on sudden to really good suggestions. Knowing Moreno had ridden in to hear most of it he turned to his self-appointed *segundo* and said, "Get your *muchachos* started on forting up. Me and some of these mining engineers will see to the illumination. I want all such chores carried out before dark. So we'd best get cracking."

They did. By the time the whole sky was a star spangled bowl of ebony Longarm and a couple of squareheads called Hans and Ludwig had planted the last unlit bonfire out along the rim of the wide expanse of bare dirt the Mexicans had cleared, cutting the stickerbrush off at root level with their machetes or shovels. When one of the Germans asked whether they might not get a serious brush fire going if and when they lit the far end of the quick-fuse inside the wagon ring, Longarm smiled wolfishly and said he surely hoped so. That inspired both Germans to smile wolfishly once they'd compared notes in their own lingo and gotten the whole picture.

Having done all he could for now, Longarm made a wish upon one star that seemed to be falling and herded Hans and Ludwig back inside the tightly circled and well dug-in vehicles. The other folk and all the stock inside had room enough, as long as everyone watched where he or she spit, or planted a bare foot.

Once he'd inspected and handed out some last advice, Longarm picked up his Winchester again and told Herr Kruger he was going back out to patrol on foot a few furlongs out, adding, "Don't shoot anybody coming in on his feet and yelling a heap. That'll likely be me."

Moreno, overhearing from nearby, asked Longarm if he wanted more pickets out. Longarm shook his head, saying, "Already considered that. No offense, but your average Mex is more likely to get his throat slit by a Yaqui than to see him by no more than starlight."

Moreno frowned and growled, "*Sin falta,* anyone can see you are a cross between an owl and a cat. So tell me, was it your father or your mother who fucked that owl?"

Longarm said, softly, "Watch that mouth. I ain't going to say that again. I've scouted hostiles for the Seventh Cav and as you see I'm still here, which is more than some of the Seventh Cav has to say for itself. I ain't low-rating your boys because of their complexions. I just happen to be good at this sort of shit."

"Modest, too," said the Mex in a tone of restored good humor as Longarm eased out through a gap between two wagons to suddenly feel lonesome as hell as he strode into the darkness alone.

He couldn't see the far side of the cleared field of fire. He knew he was there when he snagged his tweed pants on shin-high islay, a half-ass cross between a holly and a sloe bush. It was as good a place to hunker down for a listen as any. So he hunkered and listened, exploring the spiny islay leaves for a nibble as long as he was down there.

He found no fruit. It didn't upset him. Indians had the patience it took to really enjoy islay plums. Everyone else found them mostly stone with a faint hint of sweetness in the thick skins and gummy coating of pulp.

Indians liked 'em. Some desert nations even ground the stony innards of islay to a bitter half-ass meal they mixed with ground ironwood nuts, mesquite beans, and such. He wasn't sure about this far south but up Arizona way islay plums would be ripe for the picking about now. He hoped they ripened and fell off earlier in Sonora. Otherwise someone had been *picking* in these parts, recent. So where might they be, right now, if they were friendlies? Papago almost never begged and Pima were almost as proud. But a big wagon party passing through usually had tobacco, salt, and such to swap for fresh tunas, sweet saguaro syrup, or cactus butter.

The night critters all about had gotten over him being there and started to stir normal again. He slowly rose and commenced to drift, freezing in place each time something skittered or a cricket fell silent. His intent was to silently circle, not to give his own position away. White burglars and Indian raiders moved the same way. It took a mite longer to get there but the folk you were creeping in on were hardly in any hurry for your visit.

There was enough going on in the darkness all about to assure a picket worried about Indians. The chirpsome desert bugs kept saying it was a grand night for romance and Longarm's imitation of a slowly drifting saguaro allowed the little hunted and hunting critters go about their more important skitterings as if he hadn't been there. He eased out from the brush line a mite after he'd heard the anguished dying squeaks of a snake-struck kangaroo rat. It would soon be cooled off enough to discourage cold-blooded critters. Meantime the first hours after sunrise or sunset were the best times to get in trouble with rattlers or those big, beaded lizards that made up for their weaker poison by hanging on like bulldogs. Neither bit anything big as a human on purpose. So it only took a little common sense to avoid mutual misunderstandings during snake time.

He'd made it about halfway around the blacked out and fairly silent wagon circle when he heard more crunching footsteps than crickets and dropped silently to one knee, Winchester aimed the way he was listening. Then he heard a she-male voice call, softly, "Custis, *wo bist du?*"

He wasn't sure what that meant but it hardly seemed he was being addressed in any Indian dialect. So he softly called back, "I'm over here and it's a good thing for you I ain't trigger happy! Is that you, Erica?"

She allowed it was and crunched on over to him, saying, "We have to talk. My romantic nature is beginning to create a real problem for me."

He grimaced down at her dark blur and demanded, "Jesus H. Christ, can't you sort of strum your own banjo if it can't wait only another hour or less? I'd be proud to get romantic with you some more as soon as the moon comes up to tell us we're *alone* out here. Meanwhile you'd best get back inside the wagons."

She stayed where she was and said, "I'm afraid Herr Kruger knows about us and he's on very close terms with my, *ach, verlobter* in Santa Rosalia!"

Longarm sighed and said, "If *verlobter* means the same as intended I'm glad I ain't old Kruger. I ain't sure *what* I'd do if I knew a gal a good pal meant to wed was, well, no better than she ought to be. Why did you have to go and tell old Kruger about us, for Pete's sake?"

She said, "I didn't tell anyone but another *fraulein* I thought I could trust. Just now, Ynez, the servant I suspected unjustly, I fear, warned me the *chicas* of that other German girl have been making vile jests about you, me, and the difference in our height."

Longarm had to smile, knowing just about the way they'd have put it in country-gal Spanish. Meanwhile that wasn't what he'd come out here with his guns to study on. So he said, "The three fastest means of communication known to man are Telegraph, Telephone, and Tell A Woman. Since you'd gone and done it I can't tell come up with any legal way to shove the cat back in the bag. Meanwhile we got to get you to Santa Rosalia alive before we got to worry about the feelings of the poor soul waiting for you there."

He shifted the Winchester to the other crook of his arm and added, "I know you gals have a tough time grasping this, but there are times a man worries more about his ass than *getting* some. This is one such time. Even as we speak some Indians could be homing in our sweet talk with a skinning knife between his teeth. So get your sweet skin back to the wagons and wait for me by moonlight. I'll come to thee by moonlight, Lord willing and the creeks don't rise, like it says in that fool poem."

She said, "First promise to take me with you to your own country."

He said, "Hell, don't hold me to all that *moonlight* if they hit us this side of moonrise!"

Chapter 17

They didn't. The big old desert moon rose damned near full, like a partly squoze orange, to shed considerable light on the subject. Longarm stayed out on picket 'til the moon got high enough to light up all the way and dust the chaparral all the way to the horizon with silver paint. Then he said, "Well, boys, if you ain't come I reckon you ain't coming," and headed back to the wagons.

Inside, he found most of the others still tense. He announced they had every right to be, but that he didn't think it too likely they'd be hit, now. He said, "Yaqui never attack folk who can see 'em coming when they don't have to and, up until recent, they didn't have to. Them Nadene know by now that this party's too strong to take in broad day, even from ambush in hillier country. So while I suggest four or five keep an eye out in all directions, just in case, the rest of us might as well turn in for a few winks of shut-eye, hear?"

They must have heard. For they let him know in no uncertain terms they didn't think much of him right now. A younger cuss with a poor command of English began a garbled version of the boy who'd cried wolf. Knowing Longarm spoke Spanish better than German, Herr Kruger commenced to give him hell for all that wasted labor, to say nothing of the expensive mining supplies.

Speaking in the same lingo, Longarm began by calling the older man a *pendejo,* which could mean a total bastard or a stupid idiot, and added he was a *nalgason* or talking like an asshole. Then, having shut the old squarehead up, or reduced him to sputtering indignation, Longarm explained more politely, "All that quick-fuse can be salvaged to use again, the same way, when we camp the same way tomorrow night. I know I put you and your party to a lot of trouble. We're living in troubled times. I was in a war a time before this one. We had this old sergeant who'd been at it longer. It seemed every time we stopped advancing or retreating he made us clear a field of fire and dig in behind anything handy. He made us do so when even our officers said we were well behind our own lines. We were only half joking when we talked about drawing straws to see who got to murder him in his sleep. We lost count of the times he ordered us to take so much trouble for no sensible reason any of us could see. Then, one rainy night with neither moon nor stars, we saw."

He paused and lit a smoke for himself to let his earlier words sink in before he said, "It was a well thought-out night attack. The enemy came at us in strength behind a heavy artillery barrage. Some of the shells they lobbed inside out-lines were firebombs, meant to light our positions up. I'm sure they did. But we weren't positioned the way green troops camped behind their own lines were supposed to be. There was enough light coming over our shoulders to shoot the livers and lights out of the enemy skirmishers advancing on us."

Herr Kruger scowled and said, "That gives you no right to speak to me so disrespectfully. Perhaps you know more than we do about fighting. There are other questions about your morals I would like to talk to you more privately about."

Longarm nodded curtly and said, "I know what you have in mind. It can wait. Getting across this desert alive may or may not be more important to you, but at least it's a problem with an obvious solution."

Herr Kruger said he saw Longarm *did* know what that other problem was and turned away to bark some orders and shut some grumblers up in German.

Longarm couldn't follow enough of the drift to feel too interested. So he eased off along the inner wheels of the wagons, looking for Juan Moreno.

Erica Lindermann must have thought he was looking for her, from the way she grabbed hold and hung on as he was passing her two-wheel cart. She buried her face in his vest to sob, "*Ach*, Custis, take me away from these narrow-minded *heucherin*, I mean hypocrites, but first make love to me, right, in my sweet little bed. What gives them the right to gossip about me? I know for a fact that at least three of the other women have been flirting with men they should not have!"

He kissed her just enough to assure he wasn't sore at her and soothed, "They ain't hypocrites, yet, if all they been up to is flirting. You got to learn to screw more discreet, doll. I'll do my best to teach you how, later. First I got to find old Moreno."

She sniffed and told him the forward Mexican, her words, was no doubt with one or both of those Mex widows, if not molesting her maid, Ynez, again.

Longarm chuckled, pried himself and his Winchester loose, and moved on. It would have been rude to peer inside wagon tarps or down betwixt the wheels at most anyone doing most anything, so he called out, "Moreno, front and center, *cabrón*!"

It worked. The young Mex joined him a few moments later, buttoning up as he grumbled, "*Que pasa?* Can't you get your own *mujeres?*"

Longarm said, "Wanted to make sure you were still with us, for openers. After that, we may be leaving sudden. I seem to be in bad with the powers that be."

Moreno chuckled and said, "I know. You sure got into that blonde good and they say she turned down a few chances before we joined the party. I know at least two *mujeres* who have always wished for to visit your country. Why don't we just saddle four good *caballos* and ride, eh?"

Longarm said, "I'd like to light out just a tad farther from them Indians to our east and closer to the coast roads to our west. But we'd best be prepared to leave on short notice, alone, if it's all the same with you."

Moreno sighed and said, "*Mierda,* you are not my type and I had forgotten how good it felt, waiting for you in that *chingado* jail."

Longarm said, "Aside from slowing us down I don't have jail-one to put no Mex gals in once we make it back across the border. It would be dumb to put the cuffs back on you, after all we've been through and the sensible way you've been talking. But I ain't about to charge extra railroad tickets, daily rations, and such to the U. S. Justice Department. Just make sure you keep a couple of saddled ponies in reserve any time you see me out on picket, afoot. I doubt anyone will start up with me here inside the wagon ring."

Moreno whistled softly and asked, "You think some *hijo de perro* will try for to *take* you, out on the desert?"

Longarm shrugged and replied, "I'd rather run from a fight than fight a man more in the right than myself. I'm hoping it can be avoided. If it can't, I'd like to move out as the war talk's just getting serious. I doubt anyone with a bone to pick with me could be too experienced to lather himself up for a showdown before push comes to shove."

"*Ay,* Jesus, Maria *y* Jose, I had no idea anyone was that worked up over that blonde. Most of my own *raza* find your behavior amusing and, as I just said, one of those *mujeres* is for you, any time or place!"

Longarm laughed despite himself and said, "I'm already in enough Dutch, in this case, literal. Meanwhile, we'd best all catch some shut-eye, or try to, leastways."

They shook on it and parted friendly. Longarm rejoined Erica in her cart. She was already stark and she'd been right about what a swell bed she had. So what with one damn thing and another it was almost time to move on before he got much sleep that night.

Chapter 18

They broke camp just before first light, of course, and that would have still been way too late if they'd had the desert all to themselves. A wagon party perforce moved no faster than its slowest team. Ox teams on the cooler Oregon or California Trails to the north could average twenty miles a day in decent weather. Afraid to move by night and unable to move during the hot siesta hours, they hadn't made ten full miles before darkness fell and it was time to circle up and dig in again.

Nobody liked it much and "Wolf, wolf, wolf" sounded much the same in German as it did in English. Moreno was pestering Longarm to ride on and Longarm used that to browbeat Herr Kruger into forcing his followers to follow orders.

Nothing happened that night, save for Longarm agreeing they might as well break camp around four in the morning by the light of an even fuller moon with some stars already winking off to the pearly east.

They stole a few more miles that day by pushing on under an overhead sun 'til all the stock was lathered and the smarter mules refused to plod another damned step. The Mexican teamsters didn't have to be told to water generous, despite the ominous amount they had left after that much time on the desert trail without so much as a cactus to wring out. The Anglo cowhand had learned from his *vaquero* mentor just how far one could safely push livestock. Neither the *vaquero* nor his Anglo stepchild, the buckaroo, treated anything bigger than a kitten as an infernal playmate and, if anything, Hispanics could be accused of cruel and unusual punishment when a critter disputed who might be the boss. But unlike many a sweet Anglo child who wound up with dead goldfish from overfeeding or dead bunnies from overpetting, your average Mex could keep a critter alive and get more out of the same than your average biologist thought possible.

So it was the women and children, along with the less aggressive men, who suffered short water rations that afternoon as they rested and watered teams plodded on after three-thirty. Longarm, scouting out ahead on a fresh pony, found another pear flat, albeit a more modest one, a tad farther west than they'd figured to be by sundown. He rode back to the party to issue modified orders. From the way some grumbled, they were fed up with hearing any sort of orders from any damned body.

With Moreno's help, Longarm still got an advance party, mostly Mex, mounted up with their machetes and eager to slice cactus. So by the time the wagons caught up with them, Longarm's advance party had a sw/ell campsite set up with a couple of hogsheads brimming with cactus water.

There wasn't a cactus standing by then, of course. Some pads were piled to be wrung out or fed to the stock later on. But nothing a lizard could hide behind had been left standing within four hundred yards of dead center. Longarm had said as long as they had the time they might as well do it halfways right. When Moreno asked what he meant to plant on all that cleared acreage Longarm had bleakly answered, "Nadene, if we're lucky. Yaqui, if we ain't. You *muchachos* are lucky I ain't an old sergeant I used to hate. I figure four hundred yards is practical. Should the truth be known a Navy Colt can carry six hundred and your average rifle can kill at a mile. But fortunately for you-all, nobody can count on hitting shit with anything much farther out than we've already cleared.

Brush cover won't help any Indians hit by shithouse luck, so what the hell."

Most of what they'd cleared was chaparral, piled separate and hence handy to shove under the wagons once they'd been circled tight in the gathering dusk. When Longarm shouted to make sure everyone piled some solid dirt up as well, more than one shouted back in German and their word for "Mother" was close enough for anyone to follow their drift.

It was hard to say how well his suggestions had been carried out by the time it got too black to tell who was cussing you. Longarm ran the last quick-fuse out to the last brush pile along their perimeter himself. For by then he had to feel his way and didn't want to waste time asking the identity of anyone out yonder he might be feeling up.

After that, things started about the same as the last couple of tedious evenings. He circled slowly, more than once, as he listened to the chirping and skittering, waiting for that lazy old moon to get up and let him lie down. He was starting to miss that feather bed in Erica's cart more than anyone who might be in it. He hadn't tired of luscious flesh and ingenious wiggles. He even found her hot lips luscious, when she wasn't using them to beg for American citizenship. He'd told her over and over he didn't work for the infernal Immigration Department and that she didn't have to apply in Denver. She didn't seem to savvy, or didn't want to savvy, that all she had to do, if she was serious, was catch a coastal steamer north from Santa Rosalia, catch the stage from the Colorado Delta to say Yuma, Arizona Territory, and just be as American as any other English-speaking blond lady.

He told her how old Lola Montez had blown into California after they'd thrown her out of Bavaria for driving Mad King Ludwig even madder. He'd explained, "Nobody never asked Miss Lola for any proof of citizenship. Not even after she'd danced almost naked for the boys on the Barbary Coast, her charms concealed by no more than black rubber spiders, which she threw to her admirers one by one as they tossed ten- or twenty-dollar gold pieces as the dance got hotter."

Erica had pouted that she didn't want to do the spider dance in San Francisco or marry a rich *ranchero* like old Lola Montez had. He couldn't seem to convince her she didn't want to go to Denver, no matter how many times he made her come.

Thinking about that part, wishing the damned moon would rise some damned time that night, Longarm almost missed the unusual sound of no sounds at all. Then he silently sank to his haunches near a brush pile, Winchester across his knees, as he quietly groped out a match. He held his breath and, right, all he could hear for yards around was the rustle of his own heartbeat in his own straining ears. He waited, silently counting to a hundred. That was over a full minute, and no lovesick cricket had ever shut up that long without a good reason.

Longarm gripped the wax stem of the Mex match in his left fist and felt with his knuckles 'til he found the newsprint laced with black powder amid the tangle of dry twigs and branches. Then he took a deep breath, thumbed the match head alight, and was already rolling away as the brush pile flared to cast orange rays in all directions.

Hence the goggle-eyed Indian blazing away with that old Spencer missed Longarm entire as Longarm blew half his painted face off with a more accurate round of .44-40, and then they'd both dropped away from the light as guns commenced to sound off, blindly, in every fool direction.

Knowing what figured to happen next, and dreading the same, Longarm was crawling off into the chaparral on one elbow and both knees by the time the quick-fuses lit inside the wagon circle could set fire to all the other piles and light up the whole perimeter to no doubt embarrass the shit out of all those Indians out in the open on their own fool hands and knees.

As they commenced to leap up, a good many were shot right down. For a backlit man-sized target wasn't too hard to hit at that range. Some few had made it within seventy-five yards of the wagons by the time Longarm had literally exposed their nefarious plans, and they'd likely been the leaders. For those farther out, and hence in better shape to escape with their lives, proceeded to fall back.

That's when those on the north side of the forted wagons, where Longarm was, began to discover the grim way that the nearest cover was already occupied, by a mighty fine shot with a repeating rifle. Longarm dropped four in a staggered echelon as they bolted out of easy range from him, back into tolerable range from the wagons and, say what one would about German boys, they sure seemed keen on rifle shooting. Longarm had read somewhere that rifle guns were a German invention, brought to Penn State and Kentucky by them Pennsylvania Dutch, and of course that had been why old King George had hired all those Hessian riflemen in green uniforms to get even with Morgan's Virginia Rifles that time.

One Indian, whether wounded or just a free thinker, ran back toward Longarm, smack through a bonfire, to land facedown out in the chaparral with him, a .44-40 in his heart and his raggedy cotton pants brightly burning.

Some of those others were dressed more Mex than Nadene or Comanche, come to study on their sprawled forms. The one he'd just downed had been wearing a sombrero with eagle feathers stuck in the straw crown. Longarm moved closer for a better look. The dead man's face was smeared with gold paint and his hair was longer than most church-going Mexicans admired. Meanwhile his flaming pants had set the nearest clump of chamisa on fire, too. So Longarm salvaged the dead Indian's Henry repeater and eased back into the chaparral even as some asshole on one side or the other pegged a shot at the brush tops he was moving and then, off in the distance, the night was rent by the brassy sounds of a bugle, blowing "No quarter!"

No Anglo bugler had that call in his repertoire. Longarm hadn't thought that could be the U. S. Cavalry to the rescue and, by now, the fucking chaparral was lighting up all around him as other brush blazed high from the very bonfires some asshole named Custis Long had prepared without this particular eventuality in mind!

He moved back, since there was no smarter place to move, with both his depleted Winchester and the Henry that Indian had dropped close enough to get at. He was glad he had when a quartet of mounted Indians popped up from nowhere to bear down on him, screaming something about blankety blank "saltu," which made 'em Yaqui, sure enough, then dead Yaqui as Longarm opened up with both rifles, from the hip, to spill them from their running ponies.

He only had time to stare after the bolting horseflesh wistfully for a few seconds. Then someone seemed to be calling his name and he turned to see Moreno riding his way through the orange and purple smoke, leading another mount for him, Lord love such a crazy Mex, and it was still close. For the flames were dancing wildly across the crowns of the dry chaparral and blind-fired bullets were whizzing through the tricky light on bumblebee wings of death by the time Longarm was tear-assing after Moreno with one foot in the stirrup of his McClellan and the other tagging after as best it could.

Then they were loping through darker chaparral as the moonrise drew a silver horizon to their right and Moreno slowed down enough to gasp, "*Federales!* There must be hundreds of the baby-raping *pendejos cagados,* or how else could they be on the attack against *los* Yaquis, eh?"

Longarm grunted, "We knew they were out after Yaqui. It's just as well they found 'em, from the standpoint of them greenhorns."

Moreno laughed and replied, "*Sin falta, pero* all in all I did not feel it would be so nice for either of *us. So voy a joder por ahí!*"

Longarm found himself in full agreement they should go fuck around somewheres else. He felt sure Erica could always get someone to take her up to the States if she really wanted to go. As they fell into an easy lope across the desert by the light of the rising moon he called out, "By the way, *muchas gracias,* Moreno. I've had many a prisoner in the past who might have rid off by himself just now."

The young Mex laughed lightly and replied, *"De nada.* They'd have only sent someone else after me and he might have turned out a real *patada en el culo!"*

Chapter 19

Next morning they came upon a remote water hole or, in point of fact, a good-sized puddle left over from that unseasonable rain they'd just had. The water level was down a third, the water was tepid and stagnation-green. But swarming with bitty fairy shrimp and tiny tadpoles. So Longarm figured, and Moreno agreed, nothing safe for baby spade toads should poison a man or beast.

They strained the cruddy liquid into their canteens through pocket kerchiefs. The results still tasted sort of froggy but they were glad to have full canteens and well-watered ponies under them as they moved on.

Moreno was for finding the Rio Concepcíon and following it upstream most of the way to the border town of Nogales. Longarm agreed they'd see way more water and graze along that route, and it hardly seemed likely the county of Santa Cruz could be in league with those crooks in Cochise County, but anything was possible and, after that, they'd meet way too many Mex settlers, Indians pestering 'em, or *rurales* preying on both, did they follow such regular water.

So they beelined across higher and dryer ground, trying not to kick up too much dust during the cooler daylight hours and making up for lost time by moonlight.

Thanks to that recent rain, the dust wasn't bad as usual at that time of the year, and though they couldn't avoid leaving a mighty clear trail punched through the already dry surface, the mornings took a mite longer to heat up and now the usually bare stretches were commencing to turn to fairy flower gardens as what looked like dime-sized sunflowers and thimble-sized roses strove to go from bud to seed in the time it took the rich soil under the chalky caliche to dry all the way to mummy dust again. There were more kinds of these bitty blooms than even Moreno had names for. Botanists, who likely had better things to do, lumped all such unrelated elfin growths together as "Desert Ephemera."

Mexicans knew better. One bloom tasted like pickled moss and made a mighty tasty salad.

Another time, wandering through dune country bleak enough for A-rabs to get lost in, Moreno found a dusting of violets suitable for ants to admire and pronounced them "*comida de arena*" or sand food. That made more sense when Moreno dismounted and dropped to one knee to pluck some of the microscopic blooms.

They didn't pluck easy. They had roots as scaly-looking and almost as big as sidewinders. Longarm said he'd always suspected Moreno was a Digger Indian gone astray and he had his doubts about biting into a mighty serpentine vegetable, raw. But once he had, he got down on his own knees to help Moreno uproot way more of the curious roots. For they were tender, juicy, and sweet as half-ripe apples, albeit possessed of a tang all their own. Longarm suggested and Moreno agreed they ought to leave at least a few in the sand to keep a good thing going for others who might pass this way, someday. Moreno said he felt certain the patch would have grown even bigger than they'd found it before anyone else was as foolish.

Longarm insisted they stick to country just as bleak as they kept drifting north, and if they barely found enough cactus to keep their mounts going, at least they didn't run into any other human beings, good or bad, till the overcast dawn Longarm kicked the sleeping Mex awake to proclaim, "Drop your cock and grab a sock. We ought to make Arizona Territory this side of *la siesta* if we breakfast in the saddle."

They would have, too, had not they run into a *rurale* patrol where no *rurale* patrol had any sensible need to be.

The sneaky sons of bitches in their tall gray sombreros had ridden out of Santa Cruz, Sonora, about the same time Longarm and Moreno had mounted up for parts of Santa Cruz County, Arizona Territory, nobody was supposed to be inhabiting. Longarm had been aiming all along for a stretch of unfenced, unmarked border nobody was supposed to be patrolling serious. *Los rurales* hadn't been sent to patrol the border. They'd heard gossip about the Nogales del Rio rail line. So they were scouting for train robbers, on open desert, and they'd just dropped under a timber trestle to water and shade their mounts in the dry wash under it, when Longarm and his prisoner came round a bend of the same wash to rein in, uncertainly, at mighty certain range.

"Do you know any other shortcuts below the skyline?" asked Moreno dryly as the nine *rurales*, an eight-man squad with their leader, rose with sleepy smiles and all those Schofield Colt .45s.

Longarm smiled back and called out, innocently, "*Buendías, señores*. Might this arroyo lead all the way into Arizona?"

The nearest *rurale* kept his sixgun aimed politely, but nonetheless out, as he purred back, "*Sí, pero quien sabe* whether anyone here should be going there. Do you have a name or should we simply write *Gringo Chingado* on your grave marker?"

Longarm smiled indulgently and replied, "I am called Crawford because you boys have trouble pronouncing Smith. Before you put that down on any grave marker, be advised I graze me a fair-sized herd just north of here and both my old woman and a dozen riders who may have lost kin at the Alamo are expecting me home for supper."

He pointed casually to the somewhat frozen-faced Moreno to add in an easy tone, "This here's my *segundo*, Pancho. I know he's a lazy greaser but he hunts strays good. That's what we've been up to down this way. I don't suppose you boys have seen any whiteface-longhorn-cross critters, branded IB Lazy-2?"

Another *rurale* came out into the sunlight from the shade of the trestle, levering a round in his saddle gun as he called out to his comrades, "*Ay, que embustero mierda!* These are the criminals they wired us for to watch out for! El Brazo Largo and that *bandido* he was taking back to his own country for to hang, no?"

An even smarter-looking *rurale* held his sixgun up for silence as he moved closer to the two mounted fugitives as if for a closer look. Longarm murmured, "Don't," as he sensed Moreno at his side seemed ready to bolt. Longarm knew they could both ride back around the bend before the *rurales* could get to their own mounts under that trestle. But there was no way to ride that many bullets at the range both sides had to work with.

Longarm had made up his mind to go down fighting with his handier sixgun before letting the sons of bitches cuff him. But before that could happen the *rurale* with his own Colt raised so imperious stared gravely up at Moreno to demand, "If this one is supposed to be a prisoner, on his way to his own hanging, for why does he have a .45 on his hip and a Henry hanging from his saddle swells?"

The *rurale* with the rifle looked less certain, but insisted, "The gringo still answers to the description of El Brazo Largo, no?"

The surprisingly but pleasantly wrong *rurale* shrugged and said, "What of it? Can you tell one gringo, or one *chino*, from another? *I* can't. Although, now that you force me to look closer, I do think I may have seen his ugly face somewhere before."

Longarm was coming to the same conclusion. He didn't think much of the Mex's looks, either. But there *was* something familiar about the ugly son of a bitch.

The vaguely familiar *rurale* nodded soberly and declared, "He's all right, for one of them. I remember his ugly face from just the other side of the border. He may have as many friends up there as he says and he did nothing *cagado* to me when I was a guest in his country."

So while there was some mutterings about it and nobody invited Longarm and his prisoner to coffee up with 'em, they seemed free to ride on. So they did so, walking their mounts slowly under the low trestle, politely wide of the *rurales'* remuda. The only one in the bunch who'd spoken up for them seemed to be tagging along, afoot, so once they were out in the sun again on the far side, Longarm reined in to face the oddly decent cuss, saying, "*Gracias*, we owe you and, do I ever get the chance I meant to treat you as fair."

The *rurale* smiled up shyly and softly replied, "You already have. Don't you remember me? The last time we met the shoe was on, how you say, the other foot?"

Longarm hadn't done that many favors for *los rurales* in his time, or vice versa. So he didn't have to study too hard before he suddenly beamed and decided, "The El Paso freight yards. You boys, me, and some Texas Rangers were in mutual hot pursuit of a want and I do recall smoothing over some jurisdictional disputings before anyone else could get hurt."

"You did, and I said I would pay you back, someday," said the Mex lawman, slapping the rump of Longarm's pony as he added, "So go with God, El Brazo Largo!"

So Longarm and Moreno did, not looking back, as they proceeded to leave Mexico in a cloud of dust.

Chapter 20

Having already learned the hard way about the casual approach to law enforcement in remote parts of the Southwest, Longarm felt it safer to push their mounts a mite further than their luck with the law a day's ride north of the border. Moreno said he didn't care. Another day in Apache Country didn't sound much worse than the federal house of detention in Denver. Longarm had explained and Moreno had accepted with good grace the simple fact that Marshal Vail was likely to have a frothing fit on the rug the day a deputy brought a prisoner in wearing a sixgun instead of leg irons.

They made for the railroad town of Elgin, twenty-odd miles north of the border, where Longarm could send some wires and get some answers before Moreno surrendered his guns. He told the young Mex he felt no call to take further security measures, no matter what the infernal regulations said.

Moreno said he was glad and asked if it was likely they'd let him out on bail, pending his trial, once they got through all the first paperwork in Denver.

They were riding through higher chaparral along a ridge of the Santa Cruz range at the time. So Longarm made a mental note his man was most likely to bolt downhill to the east than uphill to the west as he calmly explained, "Billy

Vail's firm but fair. I reckon I can get him to put in a good word for you, once I tell him about all we've been through together. But lest you call me a big fibber, later, I can't say the court will take our word on you, old son. You *were* picked up on a fugitive warrant and the bail they're likely to set on a poor old boy facing charges of murder in the first and interfering with the U. S. Mails is likely to strain your financial resources out of sight."

He saw he was making the Mex feel morose and quickly added, "On the other hand the Constitution of these United States calls for a speedy trial as well as a fair one and our house of detention ain't so bad. They'll feed you thrice a day, nobody will get to cornhole you, and I'll see you get plenty of smokes and reading matter published in your own lingo."

Moreno sighed, said he was anxious to get it over with and that they'd likely be gunned by those crooked lawmen from nearby Soapy Wells if Apache didn't get 'em first.

They ran into neither. Longarm had chosen game trails through high chaparral with a certain amount of invisibility in mind. When they drifted into Elgin late that afternoon they gave false names at the livery where they left their mounts and told more big fibs as they wet their whistles and asked directions at the saloon across from the Western Union.

It was more usual for a lawman passing through to pay a courtesy call on the town law. Longarm told a little white whopper to the one town deputy drinking firmly and asking casual, just down the bar. It was easy enough to pass for a stockman looking for strays with his *segundo* in country where cows got lost so easy.

Once they'd established nobody in Elgin seemed all that interested in strangers of their general description, they went over to the telegraph office. Moreno sat out front, whittling, with that Henry across his knees, while Longarm went on in to send some desperately casual messages to his Uncle Billy in Denver and another uncle up at the territorial capitol who was likely to have just a mite more trouble figuring out the simple code. He had to take the chance of signing both Custis. The telegraph clerk never blinked an eye.

Longarm went back outside to sit on the steps beside Moreno, saying, "We ought to know within the hour. Marshal Vail and other honest lawmen have had plenty of time to do something about that crooked ring over to Soapy Wells if they followed my earlier drift at all. Assuming they did, we'll want to turn both ponies and that one charro saddle over to the local church charity and catch us an eastbound to ride the rest of the way in more style. I get twelve cents a mile when transporting a gent like you in for trial and the railroaders I generally run into can fix us up first class for less'n that."

Moreno asked what happened if those renegade lawmen to the east were still gunning for both of them.

Longarm sighed and said, "In that case we ain't about to take no train through Cochise County, of course. Why else would I have shoved our mounts in livery stalls and our riding gear in their tackroom?"

He glanced up at the blushing late afternoon sun and added, "Either way, we may as well get some more human food for a change. I hate to light out aboard seating provided by Pullman or McClellan on a growly stomach, don't you?"

Moreno agreed and they strode down the tracks to a sit-down *cafetin*, open all along the front and run by a lady of color who was either jolly as Hell or proud of all her gold teeth. When she told them she enjoyed a challenge and cooked any style but French, because French folk used to own her, Longarm ordered corned beef and cabbage just for the hell of it.

She never blinked an eye.

Moreno asked what they'd likely be serving him up Denver way until he explained about that other Juan Moreno to a judge and jury. Longarm said, "Mostly white bread and beans with fried eggs over hash on the Sabbath. Don't order neither. You'll get used to both after I do my best to hurry 'em up for you."

So Moreno ordered corned beef and cabbage, too. He liked it. Longarm said he never ordered grub that tasted awful. They agreed gents who could only eat strawberries out of season or unborn lamb slathered with fancy sauce at any time were likely perverse in other ways.

They were enjoying their coffee and layer cake made with ground up cactus candy when a couple of other gents came crunching along the cinder path in the tricky light, as if bound for the same cheap place to grab a bite. It was just as well Longarm had been raised polite. He'd thought nothing of two dusty strangers dressed for desert riding as they approached. He'd only started to rise from his seat because there were only three stools along the dinky counter and he was just about done. He'd meant to invite one of 'em to sit down, not to slap leather as he wailed, "Suffering snakes! It's *them*!"

Nobody born of mortal womankind could have beaten a gunslick with a lead like that to the draw. But Longarm could try as he threw himself sideways to the cinders while the bastard he'd been so polite to threw two rounds into the counter he'd just been in front of.

By this time Moreno, starting even, had beaten the other to the draw as he went over backwards the other way. So then the two strangers got to hit the cinders, further out, in far worse shape. For Moreno had gut shot his man, twice, in the time it had taken Longarm to take his own target out with a round just above the heart.

But Longarm beat the Mex to his feet and strode over to kick the gut-shot son of a bitch gently for attention as he demanded, "Who are you and how come? Speak up,'cause you ain't got long!"

As Moreno joined them, smoking gun in hand, the dying man at Longarm's feet moaned, "Don't hurt me no more. I'm hurt enough. How did you know we was here in Elgin?"

Longarm growled, "It's a gift. What's your damn name?"

The shabby stranger didn't answer. He couldn't. Longarm swore under his breath and hauled out his wallet to unpin his federal badge and stick it on his vest as he told Moreno,

"Put away that .45 and let me do all the talking. We just blew the best-laid plans of me and some mice all to hell!"

Moreno moved back under the overhang, picked up his overturned stool, and sat down to reload. The colored lady raised her graying head above the countertop to ask if it might be over. Moreno said, "*Quien sabe?* The one I was with is an honest lawman. We shall soon find out how honest your town law might be, no?"

They did. A cautiously determined old cuss with his sawed-off ten gauge at port came edging down one side of the cinder path with a pewter badge to show who he was and two younger gents backing him with four guns to indicate he meant it.

Longarm had reholstered his own sixgun and had his own hands politely out to his sides as he called out, "I cannot tell a lie. That was mostly me you boys just heard. I'd be U. S. Deputy Marshal Custis Long and I've no idea who these two dead boys might be. But they started it."

From behind the counter that colored lady called out, "I seen it all, Cap'n Wade. They was fixing to shoot that gen'man and this Mex boy, here, from *ahint*, the trashy things!"

Constable Wade moved closer, peering down at the bodies in the uncertain light of a cloudless sundown before he brightened and announced, "By Jimmies, Deputy, you just nailed Gaylord Bleeker and Jode Wallford!"

Longarm said he'd willingly do so again if only someone would tell him who he'd just shot, and how come.

The older and more well-informed lawman explained, "Big stink over to Cochise County. These two was riding for a passel of crooks who'd got control of Soapy Wells over yonder."

One of the younger town lawmen chimed in, as he holstered his two guns, "Gay and Jode, here, was about the last ones still at large. This being an election year, the incumbent sheriff of Cochise County was mighty vexed to learn they'd been shaking down merchants and robbing transients right under his nose. The smart-ass Republican running against him this time has been saying all along he ought to spend more time away from his cool, shady office in Bisbee."

Constable Wade nudged Moreno's victim with a thoughtful toe and said, "I can't help feeling sorry for this cocksucker's poor old mother. Lord knows who'll take such good care of her, now. But the Good Book warns of the wages of sin and these boys was sure sinning like there was no tomorrow. They even tried to shake down the federal government you boys ride for. Don't know the details but it sure was the last thing they *should* have done. Some big shot from the Justice Department wired the territorial government, the territorial government wired the sheriff of Cochise County, demanding some straight answers, and the rest you know."

The younger local lawman said, "There was hardly any survivors. The county riders come in spoiling for a fight and some asshole fired a shot heard round the county. We'd heard *these* two was still at large. Hadn't heard they was up this way, though. Everyone thought they'd made for Old Mexico, as bad as they was wanted."

Constable Wade said, "They must have thought you and your Mex sidekick had trailed 'em here to Elgin. Aunt Sukie just now said they tried to backshoot you. So, sure, it all falls into place and you boys stand to collect the handsome bounties Cochise County just put out on the fugitive fuckers!"

Longarm glanced at the setting sun, shrugged, and said, "My home office frowns on my putting in for blood money. My boss says it could give the impression they don't pay me enough or that I'd let a crook go if there was nothing in it for me. Yet it does seem a shame not to have some damned body get some damned good out of these otherwise worthless sons of bitches."

The old-time town constable had dealt with federal gents in the past. So he was grinning like a cat admiring a canary as he quietly agreed and allowed he was open to any suggestions that didn't sound too painful.

Longarm said, "Me and yonder *amigo* would rather catch the next eastbound passing through than mess with paper-work for your coroner and such. So we'd have no call to say different if you and your own wanted to take credit for the capture of these two."

Wade chuckled in the gathering gloom and replied, "Describing these poor brutes as *captured* could be overstating the case. On the other hand, there they both lay, well within our municipal boundaries, and if you and your Mex pard didn't end their unlawsome flight to avoid prosecution *somebody* must have!"

When one of his own sidekicks said no taxpayers of their own particular county stood to lose, in the end, Wade growled he dammit knew that. Then he shook on it with Longarm and allowed the next eastbound combination would be stopping in Elgin to jerk water in about an hour and change.

So Longarm rejoined Moreno at the *cafetin*. He paid up and left a handsome quarter tip to thank the nice old gal for her extra services. Then he told Moreno he felt no call to wait for wires when he knew what they'd say. He added, "We just got time to settle up at that livery, talk to the railroad dis-patcher about special rates and so on. So let's move out."

They did. By now the sky had gone wishing-star purple and lamp lights were winking on in the windows all about as they strode side by side along the dusty street. Somewhere in the night a guitar was sadly sobbing about La Paloma. It seemed to make Moreno pensive. But for old time's sake Longarm waited until they were alone, down near the gaping black maw of the livery, before he said, "Hold it. I didn't want to shame you in front of others, back yonder. But now that nobody's looking you'd best hand over that gunbelt, gun and all."

Moreno swung to face him, heels planted wide and sort of stubborn as he protested, "*Por que?* I thought we had a deal."

Longarm nodded soberly and said, "We did. That was then. This is now. If *I* can see we don't have to back each other against wild Indians and wicked lawmen no more, *you* can see it just as clear, so, no offense, I'd feel more comfortable escorting you the rest of the way less armed and dangerous-looking."

Moreno tried, "*Ay, hombre*, I saved your *culo* down in Sonora!"

Longarm answered, amiably, "More than once. I ain't enjoying this conversation, either, but there are limitations to how gentle I'm allowed to escort a prisoner, which you still are, and I'd look dumb as hell delivering you in Denver with that big old horse pistol on your hip, so . . ."

"On my mother's head I am innocent!" Moreno insisted.

Longarm nodded but said, "They sent me to fetch you, not to act as your judge, jury, or even your defense attorney. If I was any of them you'd likely get off. You got me half sold. But I ain't the one you got to sell your sad story to. So about that damn gun . . ."

Moreno shifted his weight and softly asked, "What if I said I would rather saddle one of those *caballos* inside and perhaps seek employment out in San Diego or perhaps *el pueblo de* Los Angeles?"

Longarm said, as quietly, "I wish you wouldn't. For that'd amount to as much as a full confession and I was sure hoping they really had that mail train blamed on the wrong cuss."

A million years went by.

Then Moreno said, "I do not wish for to kill you, Brazo Largo. Why can't you just tell them I was killed by Yaqui, south of the border? Neither those *rurales* nor these Arizona lawmen thought I could be your prisoner, right?"

Longarm shook his head and replied, "I would if I could but I can't, old son. Like I said, I ain't enjoying this at all. But they pay me to uphold the law of the land, not to enjoy myself. So, before you get worked up any more to go for that gun, I'd like you to put your gun hand up and unbuckle that rig, slow, with the other."

Moreno went for the gun instead.

Longarm had been afraid he might. It was possible to beat U. S. Deputy Marshal Custis Long to the draw when he wasn't set for it. This time, he was set for it. So he had two rounds in Moreno before the desperate young Mex could fire his single action Schofield Colt one time.

Both landed in the dust a few paces away. Still gripping his own smoking weapon, Longarm strode over, hunkered down, and numbly asked Moreno, "Aw, why did you have to go and make me do this to you?"

Moreno stared up through the gathering darkness to reply in a small, gallant voice, "Was fifty-fifty I could take you, against no chance at all if I let you take me to Denver for to hang."

That distant guitar had stopped strumming and curious voices were yelling back and forth, nearer, as Longarm gingerly opened Moreno's bloody cotton shirt with his free hand. The dying youth chuckled, coughed, and observed, "You got me in *el estómago y uno pulmón*. It don't hurt enough for to make *un vero hombre* cry. I knew you were a good shot when I saved you for to guard my *culo*. You were not bad to have on the same side, Brazo Largo."

Longarm murmured, "Neither were you. I'm sorry it had to end like this, *amigo*."

Moreno smiled up boyishly to reply, "You say *you're* sorry? *Mierda*, how do you think *I* feel?"

Then he was dead. So Longarm was back on his feet by the time old Constable Wade and some other townees joined him over the cadaver of Juan Moreno. When the older lawman saw what Longarm had wrought he said, "Now this, by the Great Horned Spoon, is going to call for some serious explaining!"

Longarm nodded and said, "I know. Let's go on over to the saloon so's I can tell such a long-winded tale sitting down."

Wade agreed that seemed a grand notion, adding, "I reckon you could use a good stiff drink after all the shooting you've been doing lately."

Longarm glanced down at the youth he'd just killed, shrugged, and said, "I had buttermilk in mind. Right now my stomach's a mite upset for some reason."

SPECIAL PREVIEW!

Introducing a magnificent new series as big and bold as the American frontier . . .

THE HORSEMEN

The Ballous were the finest horsemen in the South, a Tennessee family famous for the training and breeding of glorious Thoroughbreds. When the Civil War devastated their home and their lives, they headed West—into the heart of Indian territory. As horsemen, they triumphed. As a family, they endured. But as pioneers in a new land, they faced unimaginable hardship, danger, and ruthless enemies . . .

Turn the page for a preview of this exciting new western series . . .

The Horsemen

Now available from Diamond Books!

November 24, 1863—Just east of Chattanooga, Tennessee

The chestnut stallion's head snapped up very suddenly. Its nostrils quivered, then flared, testing the wind, tasting the approach of unseen danger. Old Justin Ballou's watchful eye caught the stallion's motion and he also froze, senses focused. For several long moments, man and stallion remained motionless, and then Justin Ballou opened the gate to the paddock and limped toward the tall Thoroughbred. He reached up and his huge, blue-veined hand stroked the stallion's muzzle. "What is it, High Man?" he asked softly. "What now, my friend?"

In answer, the chestnut dipped its head several times and stamped its feet with increasing nervousness. Justin began to speak soothingly to the stallion, his deep, resonant voice flowing like a mystical incantation. Almost at once, the stallion grew calm. After a few minutes, Justin said, as if to an old and very dear friend, "Is it one of General Grant's Union patrols this time, High Man? Have they come to take what little I have left? If so, I will gladly fight them to the death."

The stallion shook its head, rolled its eyes, and snorted as if it could smell Yankee blood. Justin's thick fingers scratched a special place behind the stallion's ear. The chestnut lowered its head to nuzzle the man's chest.

"Don't worry. It's probably another Confederate patrol," Justin said thoughtfully. "But what can they want this time? I have already given them three fine sons and most of your offspring. There is so little left to give—but they know that! Surely they can see my empty stalls and paddocks."

Justin turned toward the road leading past his neat, whitewashed fences that sectioned and cross-sectioned his famous Tennessee horse ranch, known throughout the South as Wildwood Farm. The paddocks were empty and silent. This cold autumn day, there were proud mares with their colts, and prancing fillies blessed the old man's vision and gave him the joy he'd known for so many years. It was the war—this damned killing Civil War. "No more!" Justin cried. "You'll have no more of my fine horses or sons!"

The stallion spun and galloped away. High Man was seventeen years old, long past his prime, but he and a few other Ballou-bred stallions still sired the fastest and handsomest horses in the South. Just watching the chestnut run made Justin feel a little better. High Man was a living testimony to the extraordinarily fine care he'd received all these years at Wildwood Farms. No one would believe that at his ripe age he could still run and kick his heels up like a three-year-old colt.

The stallion ran with such fluid grace that he seemed to float across the earth. When the Thoroughbred reached the far end of the paddock, it skidded to a sliding stop, chest banging hard against the fence. It spun around, snorted, and shook its head for an expected shout of approval.

But not this day. Instead, Justin made himself leave the paddock, chin up, stride halting but resolute. He could hear thunder growing louder. Could it be the sound of cannon from as far away as the heights that General Bragg and his Rebel army now held in wait of the Union army's expected assault? No, the distance was too great even to carry the roar of heavy artillery. That told Justin that his initial hunch was correct and the sound growing in his ears had to be racing hoofbeats.

But were they enemy or friend? Blue coat or gray? Justin planted his big work boots solidly in the dust of the country road; either way, he would meet them.

"Father!"

He recognized his fourteen-year-old daughter's voice and ignored it, wanting Dixie to stay inside their mansion. Justin drew a pepperbox pistol from his waistband. If this actually was a dreaded Union cavalry patrol, then someone was going to die this afternoon. A man could only be pushed so far and then he had to fight.

"Father!" Dixie's voice was louder now, more strident. "Father!"

Justin reluctantly twisted about to see his daughter and her oldest brother, Houston, running toward him. Both had guns clenched in their fists.

"Who is it!" Houston gasped, reaching Justin first and trying to catch his wind.

Justin did not dignify the stupid question with an answer. In a very few minutes, they would know. "Dixie, go back to the house."

"Please, I . . . I just can't!"

"Dixie! Do as Father says," Houston stormed. "This is no time for arguing. Go to the house!"

Dixie's black eyes sparked. She stood her ground. Houston was twenty-one and a man full grown, but he was still just her big brother. "I'm staying."

Houston's face darkened with anger and his knuckles whitened as he clutched the gun in his fist. "Dammit, you heard . . ."

"Quiet, the both of you!" Justin commanded. "Here they come."

A moment later a dust-shrouded patrol lifted from the earth to come galloping up the road.

"It's *our* boys," Dixie yelped with relief. "It's a Reb patrol!"

"Yeah," Houston said, taking an involuntary step forward, "but they been shot up all to hell!"

Justin slipped his gun back into his waistband and was

seized by a flash of dizziness. Dixie moved close, steadying him until the spell passed a moment later. "You all right?"

Justin nodded. He did not know what was causing the dizziness, but the spells seemed to come often these days. No doubt, it was the war. This damned war that the South was steadily losing. And the death of two of his five strapping sons and . . .

Houston had stepped out in front and now he turned to shout, "Mason is riding with them!"

Justin's legs became solid and strong again. Mason was the middle son, the short, serious one that wanted to go into medicine and who read volumes of poetry despite the teasing from his brothers.

Dixie slipped her gun into the pocket of the loose-fitting pants she insisted on wearing around the horses. She glanced up at her father and said, "Mason will be hungry and so will the others. They'll need food and bandaging."

"They'll have both," Justin declared without hesitation, "but no more of my Thoroughbreds!"

"No more," Dixie vowed. "Mason will understand."

"Yeah," Houston said, coming back to stand by his father, "but the trouble is, he isn't in charge. That's a captain he's riding alongside."

Justin was about to speak, but from the corner of his eyes, saw a movement. He twisted, hand instinctively lifting the pepperbox because these woods were crawling with both Union and Confederate deserters, men often half-crazy with fear and hunger.

"Pa, don't you dare shoot me!" Rufus "Ruff" Ballou called, trying to force a smile as he moved forward, long and loose limbed with his rifle swinging at his side.

"Ruff, what the hell you doing hiding in those trees!" Houston demanded, for he too had been startled enough to raise his gun.

If Ruff noticed the heat in his older brother's voice, he chose to ignore it.

"Hell, Houston, I was just hanging back a little to make sure these were friendly visitors."

"It's Mason," Justin said, turning back to the patrol. "And from the looks of these boys, things are going from bad to worse."

There were just six men in the patrol, two officers and four enlisted. One of the enlisted was bent over nearly double with pain, a blossom of red spreading across his left shoulder. Two others were riding double on a runty sorrel.

"That sorrel is gonna drop if it don't get feed and rest," Ruff observed, his voice hardening with disapproval.

"All of their mounts look like they've been chased to hell and back without being fed or watered," Justin stated. "We'll make sure they're watered and grained before these boys leave."

The Ballous nodded. It never occurred to any of them that a horse should ever leave their farm in worse shape than when it had arrived. The welfare of livestock just naturally came first—even over their own physical needs.

Justin stepped forward and raised his hand in greeting. Deciding that none of the horses were in desperate circumstances, he fixed his attention on Mason. He was shocked. Mason was a big man, like his father and brothers, but now he appeared withered—all ridged and angles. His cap was missing and his black hair was wild and unkept. His cheeks were hollow, and the sleeve of his right arm had been cut away, and now his arm was wrapped in a dirty bandage. The loose, sloppy way he sat his horse told Justin more eloquently than words how weak and weary Mason had become after just eight months of fighting the armies of the North.

The patrol slowed to a trot, then a walk, and Justin saw the captain turn to speak to Mason. Justin couldn't hear the words, but he could see by the senior officer's expression that the man was angry and upset. Mason rode trancelike, eyes fixed on his family, lips a thin, hard slash instead of the expected smile of greeting.

Mason drew his horse to a standstill before his father and brothers. Up close, his appearance was even more shocking.

"Mason?" Justin whispered when his son said nothing. "Mason, are you all right?"

Mason blinked. Shook himself. "Father. Houston. Ruff. Dixie. You're all looking well. How are the horses?"

"What we got left are fine," Justin said cautiously. "Only a few on the place even fit to run. Sold all the fillies and colts last fall. But you knew that."

"You did the right thing to keep Houston and Ruff out of this," Mason said.

Houston and Ruff took a sudden interest in the dirt under their feet. The two youngest Ballou brothers had desperately wanted to join the Confederate army, but Justin had demanded that they remain at Wildwood Farm, where they could help carry on the family business of raising Thoroughbreds. Only now, instead of racetracks and cheering bettors, the Ballou horses swiftly carried messages between the generals of the Confederate armies. Many times the delivery of a vital message depended on horses with pure blazing speed.

"Lieutenant," the captain said, clearing his throat loudly, "I think this chatter has gone on quite long enough. Introduce me."

Mason flushed with humiliation. "Father, allow me to introduce Captain Denton."

Justin had already sized up the captain, and what he saw did not please him. Denton was a lean, straight-backed man. He rode as if he had a rod up his ass and he looked like a mannequin glued to the saddle. He was an insult to the fine tradition of Southern cavalry officers.

"Captain," Justin said without warmth, "if you'll order your patrol to dismount, we'll take care of your wounded and these horses."

"Private Wilson can't ride any farther," Denton said. "And there isn't time for rest."

"But you *have* to," Justin argued. "These horses are—"

"Finished," Denton said. "We must have replacements; that's why we are here, Mr. Ballou."

Justin paled ever so slightly. "Hate to tell you this, Captain, but I'm afraid you're going to be disappointed. I've already given all the horses I can to the Confederacy—sons, too."

Denton wasn't listening. His eyes swept across the paddock.

"What about *that* one," he said, pointing toward High Man. "He looks to be in fine condition."

"He's past his racing prime," Houston argued. "He's our foundation sire now and is used strictly for breeding."

"Strictly for breeding?" Denton said cryptically. "Mr. Ballou, there is not a male creature on this earth who would not like to—"

"Watch your tongue, sir!" Justin stormed. "My daughter's honor will not be compromised!"

Captain Denton's eyes jerked sideways to Dixie and he blushed. Obviously, he had not realized Dixie was a girl with her baggy pants and a felt slouch hat pulled down close to her eyebrows. And a Navy Colt hanging from her fist.

"My sincere apologies." The captain dismissed her and his eyes came to rest on the barns. "You've got horses in those stalls?"

"Yes, but—"

"I'd like to see them," Denton said, spurring his own flagging mount forward.

Ruff grabbed his bit. "Hold up there, Captain, you haven't been invited."

"And since when does an officer of the Confederacy need to beg permission for horses so that *your* countrymen, as well as mine, can live according to our own laws!"

"*I'm* the law on this place," Justin thundered. "And my mares are in foal. They're not going to war, Captain. Neither they nor the last of my stallions are going to be chopped to pieces on some battlefield or have their legs ruined while trying to pull supply wagons. These are *Thoroughbred* horses, sir! Horses bred to race."

"The race," Denton said through clenched teeth, "is to see if we can bring relief to our men who are, this very moment, fighting and dying at Lookout Mountain and Missionary Ridge."

Denton's voice shook with passion. "The plundering armies of General Ulysses Grant, General George Thomas, and his Army of the Cumberland are attacking our soldiers right now, and God help me if I've ever seen such slaughter! Our boys are dying, Mr. Ballou! Dying for the right to determine the South's great destiny. We—not you and your piddling horses—are making the ultimate sacrifices! But maybe your attitude has a lot to do with why you married a Cherokee Indian woman."

Something snapped behind Justin Ballou's obsidian eyes. He saw the faces of his two oldest sons, one reported to have been blown to pieces by a Union battery in the battle of Bull Run and the other trampled to death in a bloody charge at Shiloh. Their proud mother's Cherokee blood had made them the first in battle and the first in death.

Justin lunged, liver-spotted hands reaching upward. Too late Captain Denton saw murder in the old man's eyes. He tried to rein his horse off, but Justin's fingers clamped on his coat and his belt. With a tremendous heave, Denton was torn from his saddle and hurled to the ground. Justin growled like a huge dog as his fingers crushed the breath out of Denton's life.

He would have broken the Confederate captain's neck if his sons had not broken his stranglehold. Two of the mounted soldiers reached for their pistols, but Ruff's own rifle made them freeze and then slowly raise their hands.

"Pa!" Mason shouted, pulling Justin off the nearly unconscious officer. "Pa, stop it!"

As suddenly as it had flared, Justin's anger ended, and he had to be helped to his feet. He glared down at the wheezing cavalry officer and his voice trembled when he said, "Captain Denton, I don't know how the hell you managed to get a commission in Jeff Davis's army, but I do know this: lecture me about sacrifice for the South again and I will break your fool neck! Do you hear me!"

The captain's eyes mirrored raw animal fear. "Lieutenant

Ballou," he choked at Mason, "I *order* you in the name of the Army of the Confederacy to confiscate fresh horses!"

"Go to hell."

"I'll have you court-martialed and shot for insubordination!"

Houston drew his pistol and aimed it at Denton's forehead. "Maybe you'd better change your tune, Captain."

"No!"

Justin surprised them all by coming to Denton's defense. "If you shoot him—no matter how much he deserves to be shot—our family will be judged traitors."

"But . . ."

"Put the gun away," Justin ordered wearily. "I'll give him fresh horses."

"Pa!" Ruff cried. "What are you going to give to him? Our mares?"

"Yes, but not all of them. Just the youngest and the strongest. And those matched three-year-old stallions you and Houston are training."

"But, Pa," Ruff protested, "they're just green broke."

"I know, but this will season them in a hurry," Justin said levelly. "Besides, there's no choice. High Man leaves Wildwood Farm over my dead body."

"Yes, sir," Ruff said, knowing his father was not running a bluff.

Dixie turned away in anger and started toward the house. "I'll see we get food cooking for the soldiers and some fresh bandages for Private Wilson."

A moment later, Ruff stepped over beside the wounded soldier. "Here, let me give you a hand down. We'll go up to the house and take a look at that shoulder."

Wilson tried to show his appreciation as both Ruff and Houston helped him to dismount. "Much obliged," he whispered. "Sorry to be of trouble."

Mason looked to his father. "Sir, I'll take responsibility for your horses."

"How can you do that?" Houston demanded of his brother. "These three-year-old stallions and our mares will go crazy amid all that cannon and rifle fire. No one but us can control them. It would be—"

"Then you and Ruff need to come on back with us," Mason said.

"No!" Justin raged. "I paid for their replacements! I've got the papers saying that they can't be drafted or taken into the Confederate army."

"Maybe not," Mason said, "but they can volunteer to help us save lives up on the mountains where General Bragg is in danger of being overrun, and where our boys are dying for lack of medical attention."

"No!" Justin choked. "I've given too much already!"

"Pa, we won't fight. We'll just go to handle the horses." Ruff placed his hand on his father's shoulder. "No fighting," he pledged, looking past his father at the road leading toward Chattanooga and the battlefields. "I swear it."

Justin shook his head, not believing a word of it. His eyes shifted from Mason to Houston and finally settled on Ruff. "You boys are *fighters*! Oh, I expect you'll even try to do as you promised, but you won't be able to once you smell gunpowder and death. You'll fight and get yourselves killed, just like Micha and John."

Mason shook his head vigorously. "Pa, I swear that once the horses are delivered and hitched to those ambulances and supply wagons, I'll send Houston and Ruff back to you. All right?"

After a long moment, Justin finally managed to nod his head. "Come along," he said to no one in particular, "we'll get our Thoroughbreds ready."

But Captain Denton's thin lips twisted in anger. "I want a *dozen* horses! Not one less will do. And I still want that big chestnut stallion in that paddock for my personal mount."

Houston scoffed with derision, "Captain, I've seen some fools in my short lifetime, but none as big as you."

"At least," Denton choked, "my daddy didn't buy my way out of the fighting."

Houston's face twisted with fury and his hand went for the Army Colt strapped to his hip. It was all that Ruff could do to keep his older brother from gunning down the ignorant cavalry officer.

"You *are* a fool," Ruff gritted at the captain when he'd calmed Houston down. "And if you should be lucky enough to survive this war, you'd better pray that you never come across me or any of my family."

Denton wanted to say something. His mouth worked but Ruff's eyes told him he wouldn't live long enough to finish even a single sentence, so the captain just clamped his mouth shut and spun away in a trembling rage.